PITTOCK MANSION

Other Books by Kelly Running

Medicine Wheel
(The Lizzy O'Malley Mysteries, Book 1)

Celtic Ties
(The Lizzy O'Malley Mysteries, Book 2)

A Lizzy O'Malley Mystery

PITTOCK MANSION

Kelly Running

Pittock Mansion

© 2019
Kelly Running

Lake Oswego, Oregon

www.kellyrunningmysteries.com

ISBN: 978-0-578-48051-0

Editing and design by Indigo: Editing, Design, and More.

This book is dedicated to my brother.

"God bless us, every one!"

—CHARLES DICKENS, *A Christmas Carol*

Contents

Chapter 1
The Body

A NIGHTMARISH SCREAM ECHOED OVER the California-quarried white-marble staircase as the lights flickered during the gala. I froze on the steps and looked at my boss, Anthony Baker, the curator at the Pittock Mansion museum, and my coworker Molly Murphy, visitor services representative. Baker sprang like a gazelle to check on the main-level guests huddled near the library, even though we had a clear view of those guests from the stairs. Molly grabbed her cell phone from her cleavage and flew up the marble steps in her kitten heels to check the upper floors. I zipped downstairs through the service hallway and toward the basement's lower passageway.

Something is terribly wrong.

The membership gala with mystery theater and dinner—Crime and Dine—was all my planning, down to the smallest and smartest details. Just moments before, I'd checked on the actors waiting in the dark-paneled library with its heavy drapes, dusty tomes, and dragon-motif fireplace. They were due to begin the play, waiting for my cue. The caterers were serving the appetizers: dill-infused poached crab and salmon tidbits, miniature Tillamook cheese–infused potato mounds, mushrooms stuffed with Oregon truffle oil and Parmesan, and roasted vegetables—carrots, green peppers, cauliflower, and broccoli—all organic.

Guests in attendance included a wealthy real estate developer with his wife, a doctor and his partner, a banker and his wife, Jonathan Applegate (chair of the board of directors for the Pittock Mansion), and other rich Portlanders, all politically connected. Each of their bank accounts had more figures than I'd ever see in my lifetime. All had seemed fine as I'd surveyed the patrons drinking champagne and nibbling on the appetizers, playbills clutched in their hands. I was coming down the stairs and was just about to announce the beginning of the theater in the wood-paneled library. I'd planned to usher any remaining guests toward the performance. This whole scene would have made Zelda and F. Scott Fitzgerald proud—it felt like it was out of *The Great Gatsby*.

So why is someone screaming at my gala? This is not part of the script.

I hustled to the downstairs work hallway, immediately spying something out of place—a bit of midnight-blue fabric protruding from the closed dumbwaiter door. I recalled seeing the same cloth on a woman guest, the real estate broker. Usually an antique tea set was settled inside the dumbwaiter; however, this mini-elevator was large enough for a person. *Why is that fabric in there?*

The gray-haired doctor, one of the gold-star members at the gala, arrived at my side. Taking charge and putting on my big-girl pants, I pried the door open. That's when everything about the night's gala transformed from glitter to grim—because inside the dumbwaiter was Allie Campbell-Stone, jeweled eye candy of the evening, still in her asymmetrical designer dress—and quite dead.

The remainder of my evening congealed like spoiled fish.

In case you don't know, I'm an emerging psychic.

After avoiding the reality of my sixth-sense gift for most of my growing-up years, I'd finally accepted that I'd inherited a talent that is hard to understand, even for me. The other thing to know is that my psychic talents emerge when I have a murder to solve, so I've pretty much fallen into crime scenes and had to climb my way out. In truth, I'd fallen hard into this one because although most of Portland knew Allie Campbell-Stone as a high-end Oregon real estate broker, I'd met her before in another capacity—and it wasn't a pleasant memory.

In Portland her picture was plastered in advertisements—on television, websites, and bus benches—with a tartan theme behind all the ads. It was catchy, using her maiden name and the Campbell plaid. I'll give her that. But I knew her as the sleep-around I'd caught with my husband in a moment of sexual climax, in *my* bed, between *my* high-count Egyptian cotton sheets.

And suffice it to say, it was the end of my marriage.

Every time I saw the plaid, I thought about the last time I saw my husband naked—and it wasn't with me. Of course, that reminded me that my husband died when he tried to kill me, before the divorce was final, technically making me a widow.

And Allie Campbell-Stone was here, again disrupting my life and now my job too. I knew her murder at my workplace didn't bode well for me. She was dead and I didn't like her, but I wasn't the one who killed her. Whoever had done it had a strong motive, or had been short on self-control, or maybe both.

Someone at the gala killed her.

Slipping away from the crowd growing around the body, I speed-dialed my Uncle Callaghan, a powerhouse Portland attorney. I found an out-of-the-way place among the janitorial closet brooms, mops, and extra toilet paper, where I started to fall apart emotionally—a complete switch from my usually well-kept professional persona—and waited for Callaghan to pick up the call.

"Uncle? It's Lizzy. I found Allie Campbell-Stone dead in a dumbwaiter."

After a long pause, he said, "I remember the prior circumstances."

"The good news is that people were standing next to me when she screamed—and before I found her body—so I have an alibi," I said.

"Call me if anything problematic occurs. And remember, the rich have the most to lose."

My uncle. Calm, cool, collected, philosophical. The perfect high-powered Portland attorney.

To be truthful, I expected to be fired the next day. I was still in the job honeymoon period, and I'd only gotten this job on a recommendation from a friend of a friend of a friend, since Portland's job market was harder than Oregon basalt. With all the people moving into Stumptown—Portland's nickname—it was downright cutthroat.

Now, I was anxious about the review of the dinner party evening, given that the murder mystery had turned into a real murder. But what happened when I went to my boss's office the next day surprised me.

Jonathan Applegate, the *head* of the Pittock Mansion board of directors, was sitting in curator Anthony Baker's chair, looking polished and professional. Looking around, I saw that everything of my curator boss's belongings had been plucked away like autumn leaves from trees on the estate's grounds. *Curator Baker fired?* I was even more astonished when Mr. Applegate handed me the set of keys that would open every door to the Pittock estate.

He had deep ridges in his now-furrowed brow. "Ms. O'Malley, you're now interim curator *and* theater event planner. Think of it like a stage production. Juggle. Run the house like a Broadway play." Producing an airline ticket and a Caledonian train ticket, he laid both on the desk in front of me. "I need you to retrieve items for a new gate lodge exhibit."

The building he was referring to, the gate lodge, was part of the original property. The first caretaker of the mansion had been a Scot by the name of Skene who'd lived in the servant house with his family.

"I'm going to Scotland?"

"Yes, and once in Inverness, you'll see Angus MacDonald, the museum curator there. He'll have all the paperwork and logistics for what you'll need for the transfer of the antiquities."

"Inverness, Scotland?"

Pinch me. I've got an all-expenses-paid business trip to the Scottish Highlands.

"Of course. As theater people like to say, the show must go on."

This day couldn't get any better.

Chapter 2
Inverness, Scotland

MR. APPLEGATE'S PLANE TICKET FLEW me into Heathrow Airport in London, where a cabdriver took me to Euston station to make my train connection. I had time to kill while waiting for the overnight express to take me to Scotland, so after lunch at a café, I whittled away the remainder of the afternoon sipping on soda and snacking on free food in the first-class Caledonian lounge. At about eight thirty in the evening, I boarded the train and found my tiny berth in car B, number 26. I dropped off my backpack with my change of clothes and made my way to the dining car, where a spot was reserved for me, and I ordered a miniature bottle of red wine and supper.

After that, it was an almost sleepless but uneventful night.

In the early hours of the morning, the porter delivered the breakfast to my sleeper car— hot coffee, fruit, granola, and a thick Greek yogurt. After breakfast and exiting the train station, I collected a map of Inverness. I like the feel of paper in hand when I'm navigating a new city. The museum was within easy walking distance, and I'd packed light, using my ultralightweight travel backpack.

Once you've worked at a museum, you get a feel for the kind of people who work at any museum. It's usually an underpaid job that attracts top-notch people who love history and all the old things. I introduced myself to a greeter at the door, most likely a recent graduate from university, and was directed up the stairs to the curator's office.

The curator, Angus MacDonald, was in his midfifties with a gray beard and hair, dressed in neatly pressed slacks and a plaid jacket. He wore a white shirt, a sporty green tie, and silver cuff links. He got down to business as soon as I settled into the chair across from his desk and presented him with my identification.

"Items to be personally collected by a representative of the museum. I understand that the Skene family lived in the Pittock gate lodge," MacDonald said.

"Yes, Mr. Skene took care of all the property around the house, the greenhouse, and anything mechanical that needed repair. What are the artifacts?"

"We're turning over to you a traditional Highland quaich and a matched set of eighteenth-century dueling pistols, along with the dueling accessories."

I know dueling pistols, but what's a quaich? Rhymes with squish *but with a* q. *Quaich.*

He read my puzzled expression. "A quaich is a shallow cup. When filled with Scotch whisky, it was passed as a gesture of peace and goodwill."

He brought out a dark velvet bag and extracted an amber-stained wooden cup. Taking it in my hand, I traced my finger over the edges of it and felt a faint design—maybe a letter *S*—carved in the handles on both sides of it.

"It's brilliant," I said, but just as suddenly, my psychic psychometry was activated. This is my strongest psychic ability, where I can feel the emotions and sometimes even sense the owner of an object because their energy lingers. What I felt now was anger, jealously, and lust. It was like holding something too hot to handle. I set it on the desk, startled. Since I needed to attend to the business at hand, I attempted to quiet my psychic mind, intent on the historic information the curator could give me.

"I have all the required paperwork you'll need for the transfer of the goods, including a locked case for the dueling pistols, required for the travel." It appeared that everything had been arranged prior to my arrival. "How much do you know about the Highland history?" he asked.

"I have to admit, not a lot."

"I'd suggest that you start by looking at our display upstairs. There are several examples of quaich cups, both in wood and silver. And if you have the time, explore Culloden Battlefield outside of town. There's an interpretive center there, and you can also walk the moor, the site of the great Highland battle. It would give you a profound sense of Scotland's history."

Walk the moor.

Some Scottish fresh air sounded good.

Out on Culloden Moor, the wind tugged at the blue flags that marked the spots where clans had stood, some with hundreds of men, but it hadn't taken long for over a thousand Highlanders to die that day, April 16, 1746. I walked past the markers of Cameron, Stewart of Appin, and Fraser, and when I got to a stone marked as Mackintosh, I sat on a bench to release my travel weariness and the foreboding sense that something was going to happen, but I wasn't sure what.

I closed my eyes. There wasn't another soul on the battlefield. I counted that a blessing and was grateful that the Scottish weather held off from drenching me. While my eyes were shut tight, I imaged Highlanders congregated on the battlefield; however, I was surprised when I reopened them and actually spied a man in a kilt with a sporran, cap, and dirk (a really pointy knife). When the Highlander came closer, I could see the shadows of the marshy moor through him.

My pulse pounded.

Now, I've had stones whisper to me in Ireland. I've heard the murmurs of dead relatives waxing poetic and giving me advice from a Belfast cemetery. I've even seen a banshee, but this was the first time I'd ever seen a battlefield ghost.

He was standing in the godforsaken moor—surrounded by rough brush and ice-cold pockets of water—and I felt a chill like someone was walking over my Aunt Thelma's grave. The air was filled with a current of energy—like electricity but different. All the while, I wanted to mentally grab on to something tangible, something that made more sense than the fact that I was encountering a Highland spirit.

All my other senses activated—I could smell cannon smoke and the acrid scent of fear. A microchip that I'd had embedded under a tattoo grew hot. I absently rubbed my lower back where the green Celtic knot was tattooed—it marked the chip's location in case I needed it. After all, it was purported to hold information about a treasure of a famous Irish pirate queen that I'd agreed to keep safe from renegade Irish factions, but who knew if I'd need to remove it someday?

I instinctively closed my eyes again to recalibrate my sixth-sense energy. When I reopened them, the Highlander ghost was still in

front of me—so close, in fact, that I could see days' growth of whis-
kers on his well-chiseled face. I used my psychometry to tap into the
emotions of this hallowed ground. I heard the gasps of fading life,
the loss on the battle line, and the hollow echo of a final prayer to
a loved one—the most intimate moments in the last seconds of life.

The temperature dropped, and the Highland ghost came
closer—the only way I could explain the climate change—as I heard
the faint echo of bagpipes. He reached out and took my hand into
his, and at the precise moment that he touched me, he disappeared.
All that remained was my exhausted psychic state and the name *Mac*
as it came to me like a distant whisper in the Scottish wind.

I had an evening and part of one day before I would leave for my
overnight train ride to London. Looking for a place for a meal,
I was in downtown Inverness, close by the walking bridge over the
River Ness. There's a very, very old church with a churchyard cemetery on this side of the bridge. The black wrought iron gates of the
cemetery were open, welcoming. Some might say that I'm drawn
to these psychic places, the last resting place of people who lived,
breathed, and loved. I'm reverent of the history and the people who
came before me.

I wandered through the cemetery, waiting for some whispers
from the occupants underground, but I only detected the wind,
the seagulls, and a sense of peace. After reading names on several
of the markers, I looked toward the edge of the graveyard and saw
my Highland ghost.

At this point I was curious. Mac obviously wanted to show me
something. There was another marker stone in the space between

the trees, and it bore a notch with a V shape. Mac pointed at the stone, and I knew it had a message. I closed my eyes and placed my hand on it.

My psychometry flashed as I saw the execution of a man. My heart thumped, and I resisted the urge to pull away. It was a violent vision, and empathy welled into my heart, for I was aware that this was someone Mac knew, a fellow clansman who had escaped from Culloden only to be hunted down by government enforcers and killed on this spot.

I took my hand off the stone, and Mac reached out his hand, like he had done at Culloden. Though I was filled with compassion for the Highlander's spirit, I also knew that he needed to find his way back to that Highland battlefield. I wished it to happen, and he disappeared. Feeling a bit of relief, I made my way to the walking bridge over the River Ness, pausing briefly to watch the fast-moving water and seagulls perched on a small sandy beach downstream as I crossed over. From there I walked three blocks along the waterfront and stopped when I saw an eatery, the Water's Edge.

Inside, there was one patron at the bar. I was seated at a table with a view of the river outside, watching people moving past me on foot and bicycles. When the server came over, I decided on the fish dinner. I wasn't disappointed. The salmon was perfect, flaky to the fork, rich in flavor. I indulged in a large glass of pinot gris, and my cheeks blossomed pink from the wine, the warmth of the pub, and the afternoon of wind I'd walked through on Culloden Battlefield.

When I got back to the B & B for the night, I took a hot shower and had a towel wrapped around me when Mac materialized again, this time lounging on my bed, and looking…lustful. "Listen, Mac," I said, feeling out of sorts at this third visit, and in my private room. "I'm almost naked. This is not working for me."

The response was a glowing smile from Mac.

"Get lost, now!"

He reached for my hand, and something spiked through me—it was sensual energy—and then he vanished. I found myself blushing at the encounter.

I put on my nightgown, and thought I'd try some reading to relax. I slipped under my covers—after overfluffing the comforter—and reached for my book. I'd picked up an Agatha Christie paperback at the airport, *Murder on the Orient Express*. I was getting sleepy reading about Poirot's investigation—calling the members of the train into the dining car one by one—and thinking, *If only things were so easy at the Pittock Mansion*. My final thought before I closed the book and turned out the light was that I needed to shop because I love retail therapy.

Cashmere. Or jewelry. Or maybe both.

Chapter 3
Porridge and a Ghost

BREAKFAST WAS PORRIDGE IN THE B & B dining room. It was thick and rich, made the way I'd been able to get it only in Ireland and Scotland. It was loaded with drizzled honey and sprinkled with fresh fruit, and I wanted to know why it was so much better here than in Oregon. When my host came to check on me, I gushed about the creamy richness of the porridge. "What makes it taste so much better in Scotland?"

"*Emm,* do you have steel-cut oats?"

I enjoyed the filler word in Scotland—sounds like *em* instead of the American *um.* "Yes," I said, "but it doesn't taste the same."

"Do you cook it in milk?"

Ah, is that the secret to the creamy texture and taste?

"You've got to cook it in milk."

And there the mystery about good oatmeal was solved.

After checking out, I took a final walk over the pedestrian bridge and stopped to look at the view of the Munros—the mountains—in the distance, covered with snow. It was cold, and I wrapped my jacket tighter around me as I watched the seagulls on the sandy patch of beach, never appearing to leave. I had the quaich and dueling pistols safely tucked into my backpack, and now I needed retail therapy; however, when I got into the core of town—Inverness is not a very big city—I was distracted by a man in a kilt. This man wasn't faded. He was answering questions for tourists in front of the visitors center, so I asked him where I could get information about the different plaids and clans. He suggested that I head to the Inverness Library, located directly behind the bus station, only a few blocks away.

I temporarily postponed my shopping—out of character for me—to mull over some of Scotland's history books in the library. Walking uphill and then taking a left, I found the stoic building behind the buses queued up to take people to Glasgow or Edinburgh.

Inside, a librarian showed me a stack of books, and I found six or seven titles that looked promising. I dropped my heavy backpack to the side of a chair and began reading about the clans and Scotland's history. When I got to the Mackintosh section, I scrutinized a sketch of a Scottish Highland warrior who looked like Mac. Same plaid, duplicate kind of sporran. I looked for a name, but it was a generic drawing. Flipping further through the pages, I saw the plaid for the MacDonald clan—the Inverness curator's name—and the plaid that Allie Campbell-Stone had used in her real estate advertising.

I read further that the Campbell clan didn't support Bonnie Prince Charlie. As a result of what happened at Culloden, the Campbells were rewarded by the government, whereas the Jacobite clans faced starvation and death after the battle. Some Jacobite Highlanders got away and then immigrated to America, but members of the Campbell clan were cursed, still a well-known fact in the Highlands. *Allie Campbell-Stone had a curse on her family name.*

When I came up for air, my stomach was rumbling. I needed the basics: lunch and cashmere shopping. Then, I had to check in to the train station for my overnight trip to London.

The Caledonian sleeper train was parked on the tracks at eight thirty, and I entered with my railway pass. Finding my little room, I put my things inside of it—except for the artifacts and my wallet, because I couldn't lock the door for my sleeper compartment unless it was from the inside. From there, I made my way down the tiny aisle to the dining car, where I found a table reserved for me. I took a seat by the placard O'Malley, and a porter came to take my beverage order. I decided on wine—a red. After a few sips, I relaxed. I felt that I'd made progress and had a successful business trip. And I had a new cashmere scarf around my neck in a plaid of pinks and gray.

Retail therapy is brilliant.

The nice thing about being away from the mansion was that it gave me some clarity. Problems didn't seem as significant now that I was on a train, chugging through the Scottish countryside, but I knew that the honeymoon feeling would be over when I was back at the Pittock Mansion. I ordered the macaroni and cheese—I wasn't game for the haggis. Anyway, the food was surprisingly good, and with the heavy carb load and the red wine, I expected to get some sleep. Back in my tiny personal sleeper car, I spritzed it with the complimentary lavender mist, put on the free comfy socks, slipped in the gratis earplugs, and hoped for the best. Of course, about an hour after sleep failure, I needed the toilet at the end of the railway car. Returning to my room, I discovered Mac on my bed.

Now this has to stop.

"Mac," I said, my voice coming out at least an octave above normal. "You're a ghost, and you belong in Scotland!"

I really didn't know if he could disappear and regain his ghostly presence on the moor of Culloden Battlefield, but now the train had stopped at a station and was switching tracks with a jarring motion that wiggled the train at the junction. There was another abrupt shaking, and I almost fell into his lap. "Listen," I said, a little more softly, as a snore coming from the compartment next to mine reminded me of the vents joining the rooms. "I think it's better if you stop following me."

Mac looked protectively at the door. That's when I was startled by a knock and a voice. "Porter here. Did you need assistance?"

I hadn't rung for the porter even though I'd seen the switch for it if I needed him. It occurred to me that maybe he'd overheard me yelling at Mac. "No, thank you," I yelled out.

"I have bottled water," he offered.

At this point, it felt like a welfare check. I was thirsty, so I unlocked the door and let him step inside.

He took a few steps into the compartment and then stopped, handing the water bottle over to me. "It's very cold in here," he said, stifling a chill. "I'll see if I can get some heat directed toward your compartment."

"Oh, don't worry about it," I said. "I like it cold."

I didn't, but I knew who was making the compartment feel like an iceberg.

Turning toward Mac after the porter left, I whispered, "Listen, you make the temperature drop about twenty-five degrees. People might not be able to see you like I can, but if they have half a brain and some sixth sense, they are going to *feel* that you're in a room. Now, get off the bed," I whispered. "I'm really tired, and if you're not going back to Culloden, you're sleeping on the floor."

Listening to the *clickety-clack* of the train—even with ear-plugs—I looked down on the carpet at my handsome Highlander ghost, sound asleep, and detected a grin on his face. Well, at least I thought he was smiling. It's hard to tell when it's a ghost. And some relationships are difficult. Mac and I were headed in that direction.

Chapter 4
Underground Tunnel

I was able to check the artifacts in with my luggage and carry my backpack through security to the gate. After the ten hours of air from London to Vancouver, British Columbia, to Portland, I claimed my luggage without a hitch and caught a cab. It was raining, not the usual kind of grim, gray rain, but the torrential downpour where the accumulation is recorded in inches. I'd let Mr. Applegate know that I needed an extra day on both ends of my trip to take my dog, a black Labrador named Karma, to a friend's house at the coast for dog sitting and then pick her up after I got back from Scotland.

The cab pulled up in front of my apartment, and there was a new sign staked into the grass. It declared that my apartment building was to be a future condominium development by none other than Mr. Crookshank, the developer who had dined at the Pittock Mansion the night of the gala. I'd read in *Willamette Week* that he was buying property up all over Portland and spiking rents, and artists and original Portlanders were moving out because they were having a hard time making ends meet.

This didn't bode well for my renting future.

Inside my apartment, I flipped on the floor lamp and went into the kitchen for a nightcap. I hoped for a sound night's sleep before hitting the road to the coast in the morning. Opening the cupboard, I spied a bottle of Scotch. I poured two fingers into a glass and flopped on the sofa. I tried to relax, but something was bothering me, and it wouldn't stop. It had to do with the night of the gala and a rumor I'd heard floating around the mansion. Some of the volunteers believed there was a forgotten entrance to the mansion, a tunnel. When I'd first heard about it, I'd asked Mr. Baker, and he'd soundly tamped it down as fiction. Thinking about the possibility that the curator had been wrong or lying, I finished my dram and went to bed. I felt myself drifting to sleep when the microchip began to burn. Opening my eyes, I spotted the muted plaid kilt of a Highlander on my bed, next to me.

"Mac," I whispered, "get off the bed. You need to sleep on the floor."

This is getting complicated.

I stopped at a drive-through Starbucks in the morning and then hit the road to retrieve Karma. Driving's a good time to think, but I tried to avoid thoughts about Allie Campbell-Stone's murder. Instead I ruminated on why I'd spent so much of Aunt Thelma's estate money. But as soon as I turned down the quiet main street in Manzanita, I remembered that paying to keep Aunt Thelma's house was worth every penny—I would always think of this place as my home.

At the deli market on the main street, I ordered my favorite sandwich—a concoction of turkey, cranberry, stuffing, cream cheese, and romaine lettuce nicknamed the gobbler, which could take care of a single person's Thanksgiving or Christmas dinner if you added a glass of white wine. Today I added a Diet Coke, and after talking to my friends and catching up on the newest small-town gossip, I made my way to the sheriff's office to see Trinity, who was my canine's human companion when I was away.

Trinity hugged me as soon as I got through the door at her workplace at the sheriff's office. "Griffin's at a conference in Seaside," she said. "But I told him about your trip to Scotland." It still surprised me that Trinity and Sheriff Griffin kept up on my well-being even though I was spending very little time in Manzanita.

"I can't stay," I said. "Got to get back to work."

"What's the matter?" she asked, attuned to my mood by her own fourth-generation Cajun and Creole background. Her ancestors from New Orleans practiced their own forms of magic.

Whatever I told Trinity would be relayed to Griffin, and I didn't want to have to start explaining about quaich cups, Culloden ghosts, and dueling pistols, although I knew he'd be interested in the latter. I wasn't ready to share my story about Mac, even though Trinity and Griffin accepted my sixth-sense stories.

"Ah, nothing," I said as I snatched up the key that Trinity had set on the counter and thanked her.

Trinity grabbed me by the hand as she took a pouch out of her desk. She handed it to me; it was crafted out of red flannel. I felt a bump inside and knew it was a gris-gris—an amulet to keep me safe.

"Keep this with you," she said.

I gave Trinity a hug and left to pick up my dog.

When I got back to Portland, I dropped Karma at the apartment and turned my attention to the Oregon Historical Society for some fact-finding before I had to go to work the next day. Accessing the reference elevator to the fourth floor, I really didn't know what Pittock history I was looking for. I signed in to the logbook and asked the reference librarian for everything Pittock related from their archives, especially anything from the building of the mansion, its construction, and its infrastructure.

I didn't get excited until I found a volume of oral history collected around 1980. These were interviews from some of the descendants, including one from the niece of Georgiana Pittock, who had lived in the house for a short time. She talked about the old house and described a secret compartment in the dining room. I didn't know about it, and it piqued my interest. Was it large enough to walk inside? Had someone been hiding in the house, waiting to commit a murder?

Peter Gantenbein, the grandchild born in the mansion and one of the last to live there, reported that he moved into his grandfather's bedroom sometime after his father had died. He also talked about a trail by the porte cochère before the City moved the road to its current location. That made sense, because when I'd once peered over the edge of the rose beds to get a better view of Mount St. Helens, I'd seen the abandoned columns that seemed to lead to nowhere, overgrown with vines. When I'd asked Anthony Baker about it, he'd shrugged and said it's just the way it was.

Not so much, Mr. Baker. Because Peter Gantenbein described a grotto where he could go and be alone with his thoughts. The configuration of the landscape had changed a lot since the 1960s, along with memory of it. I recalled in Anthony Baker's office a photograph of workers standing by the slabs of stone cut on the site.

After sifting through all the interviews and taking some notes, I made my way to the SmartPark garage on 10th Avenue. I was considering going back to my apartment and calling it good for the day when a call came from Eric Thomson, who was the newest director at Lakewood Center for the Arts in Lake Oswego. Two actors who had been at the mansion the night of the murder had something to tell me, given that they knew I dabbled in all things psychic and that I had discovered Allie Campbell-Stone's body. Eric confessed that it was gossip in the theater community.

For background, Eric and my brother, Ryan, are friends. Eric had given me one of my first theater jobs in Portland. Ryan was building a successful theater community in Sedona, Arizona, which was where I'd gone to work after I'd found Allie Campbell-Stone in bed with my husband.

I pulled out into the flow of traffic and was startled by a fleeting image of a man riding a unicycle with a bagpipe in his hands, flames shooting out of the pipes, all while dressed like Darth Vader.

At that precise moment, Mac materialized next to me. He looked even more solid this time. He pointed at the unique character who made Portland his home.

"Don't worry, Mac. It's the Unipiper. He entertains this way."

Eric met me at the top of the stairs at the entrance of the theater and ushered me backstage, where the cast and crew were making the last of the preparations for the *1776* dress rehearsal. By that year in history, the Jacobite rebels had been through the slaughter at Culloden, and many who survived had landed in America for a second chance at life. Some became advisers to George Washington. I could've written that play if I had more time, but I had more than enough on my plate with the mansion and murder.

Two of the actors, Helen and Owen, huddled together in the front row of the vacant venue. I knew both of them from working the drama circuit.

"What do you remember that you wanted to tell me?"

"Well, we were about to use the back stairs when I saw that the service door was propped open. I didn't think much of it because I thought the caterers were bringing in supplies from their van," Owen said. "That is, until you discovered the body."

"Did you tell the police?"

"Yes, that night. I told them someone could have slipped into the mansion."

I turned toward the other actor, Helen. She could have been responsible for the fall of Troy. Blonde, perfect figure, great teeth—every costume she wore looked great on her. "And there was something we discovered," she said.

"What?"

"Under the entrance, through the garden, there's kind of a path. It's hard to see, but we went to find a place to smoke," she said. This wasn't surprising. Since cannabis had become legal in Oregon, people were taking weed smoke breaks at nearly every play, gala, or other artsy event. "I was a wreck after the police interviewed us, so we followed it along to the edge of the forest where it's heavily overgrown."

I was so excited for new information, I had to remember to breathe. "And?" I encouraged.

"There's a retaining wall with graffiti and a boarded-up panel covering a section of it that might conceal a tunnel."

With the service door propped open during the gala, anyone could have slipped into the mansion. This wasn't a closed-room investigation at all. And if there was an abandoned tunnel to the house, anyone could have also entered through an unknown passageway and killed Allie Campbell-Stone.

This is getting more complicated.

Chapter 5

Psychic Friends

THERE WAS A CHILL IN THE AIR from the storm that had denuded copious amounts of leaves from the oaks and elms. Karma had roused me for her evening kibble, and after she'd eaten, I'd clipped on her leash. By the time we'd walked down Burnside Street, I had worked up an appetite. Of course, Karma was always hungry because she's a Lab.

"What kind of food do we want?" I asked her. She wagged her tail, and in dog, that means, *Anything you eat*—Korean barbecue, Thai, Vietnamese, Reuben sandwiches.

Karma sat while I scanned the food carts for my choice. That's when I felt a tap on my shoulder and was surprised to see Peace Jones, psychic and alien chaser. The last time I'd seen her was in her crystal and new age shop in Sedona, Arizona. Before that, she'd graduated from Portland's Reed College, celebrated at the college's annual Renaissance fair, drunk from the fruit punch, and played on the naked Slip 'N Slide. The punch was laced with LSD. That's when she saw her first UFO and found alien portals for psychic communication.

"Seeing many UFOs?" I asked.

"Double. Triple. There's a galactic portal poised in a cosmic shift. Have you felt it?"

"Not so much."

"Are you going to get something to eat?" she asked.

"You bet," I said, remembering how hungry I was now that I'd met a good friend.

I decided on the Vietnamese, and Peace bought the Korean barbecue. Karma stood, watching, in case we dropped anything.

"Are you living in Portland or visiting?" I asked as we caught up on our lives.

"Came for a Reed College reunion and decided to stay for a while."

I could confide my sixth-sense questions with Peace. "I need some advice," I began. "There was a murder where I work—at Pittock Mansion, the museum. One of the guests at a gala I was hosting." I dropped my voice. "I didn't get any premonitions or any of my usual psychic warnings—hairs raised on my arms, metallic taste in my mouth. But then I was promoted to interim curator along with my job as theater and event planning manager for the mansion, and sent to Scotland for business."

We were interrupted by sirens—police cars and fire trucks—driving by.

When I turned around, Peace was gone. I was perplexed. Peace should have been easy to spot, as she was wearing a bright-purple T-shirt with the words *UFO HUNTER* stenciled in white with a silver saucer spaceship. Maybe she had seen something that caught her interest and walked away while I was distracted by the sirens?

Looking around, I spied a woman nearby staring at me over her taco. She looked uncomfortable, so I decided to bring the nonverbal communication into the daylight. "Did you see the woman I was talking to? In a purple shirt?" I asked.

She nodded and said, "Behind you."

"Where'd you go?" I asked Peace when I turned around and she'd reappeared.

"I was summoned to an important alien caucus. Some species can't be kept waiting. Did you know that you're emitting a new kind of frequency?"

The lady with the taco got up and moved away from us.

Peace was the most accurate psychic I'd ever met, even more tuned in to the sixth sense than my Aunt Thelma or Nora, my relative on the Beara Peninsula in Ireland.

"I got a tattoo—"

"And?" she prompted.

"It has an RFID chip embedded in it, a radio frequency identification device. It holds data, and mine has something to do with a treasure in Ireland. I'm the keeper of the chip so the wrong people don't get it."

"Well, your chip is like a shining star on the top of a Christmas tree. You've hit a home run to attract ghosts and other paranormal, so be prepared."

"Yeah, I think it's already done that."

I quickly filled her in about Mac manifesting in my apartment.

"Tell you what," she said, reading my tense body language at the part about kicking Mac out of my bed and the feelings of gloom surrounding Allie Campbell-Stone's murder, "I'll come up to the Pittock Mansion, and I'll let you know what's going on there—there's a possibility of a residual echo from the events of that evening. As far as your Scottish ghost, there's a reason why he appeared. After all, it was a battlefield, and you only conjured one ghost. When are you going to work next?"

"Tomorrow."

"I'll be up then. But for now, I'm still hungry. For dessert, let's get some of those doughnuts that people like to carry around like jewels in pink boxes."

"Voodoo Doughnuts?"

"The frosted ones with the cereal sprinkled on top."

Chapter 6
Paranormal Vibes

MOLLY WAS INSIDE THE THIRD-FLOOR OFFICE when I arrived, and I quickly set about confirming the count for the till to open admissions for the day. She offered me a quick congratulations on my promotion, and I thanked her. The museum store and admissions, in the former three-bay estate garage, were down the path from the house. The store would open in a half hour, and we were short on staff, a constant problem, so I planned to work the register. Molly took her walkie-talkie and the till money and left for the admissions bay while I counted out the ones, fives, tens, and twenties, plus twenty dollars of change for the store. In another fifteen minutes, we had two volunteers coming, one as greeter and the other as a tour guide.

The morning was peaceful.

Around lunchtime—after I'd dusted the shelves in the store for what must have been the twelfth time, since it was a slow morning in the store—Molly came over after she'd locked up the admissions bay and went for lunch while I covered for her and sold admission tickets from the store. When she was finished eating, we flipped and it was my turn to have a bite. My sense was that Molly was a bit of an introvert anyway, so she didn't seem to mind eating by herself. I'm more an extrovert; however, I was ready to relish the quiet of a half hour of lunch to myself.

Inside of the mansion on the third floor next to the office (formally Mr. Henry Pittock's study, where the *Oregonian* newspaper owner and editor would go to work and to get away from his family), there's a tiny kitchen space that holds a microwave, an original mansion sink, and a small refrigerator. After grabbing my sack lunch from the refrigerator, I went back to the office where we had a small conference table where we could eat and sat down. I was into my second bite of lunch when I heard a voice. Sound travels wacky in the mansion—and each floor has its own personal acoustics. The mansion was built in what I'd best describe as a horseshoe shape. When I turned around, I confirmed that the voice belonged to Peace, but before I could even say hello, she was off—a woman on a psychic mission.

"We've got spirit activity in the room next door," she said as she nodded toward a rarely used room where antiques were stored by the former curator. "And a ghost is over there by the elevator door."

I left my lunch behind and followed Peace around while she psyched out ghosts with her sixth-sense gift. Peace was now pointing to the original Otis lift, but I didn't see a ghost.

"I don't see anything over there," I said.

"I smell her. She's wearing cheap Paris perfume."

Now that was something I hadn't considered. A ghost might not manifest by sight, but nonetheless he or she might be there, the presence detected and noticed by the smell. Since it was perfumed, I assumed it was a woman. "It could be Lucy, or another of the daughters…or it could be one of the nieces." My mind was flooded with the genealogy of the Pittock family. "It was a pioneer brood. There were lots of children, although some passed early in life. Or could it be Allie Campbell-Stone?" I said this with a gasp at my realization.

Peace set her hand on my right shoulder. "We have more spirits than I expected. So we'll have to come back when there aren't so many other living energies present." She nodded toward Henry's terrace, where we could see a group of tourists making their way toward the entrance. "They are interfering with the process. I'll meet you here again about nine tonight to follow up with this gaggle of ghosts."

"The park bureau locks the gate. We can't drive up."

"Wear your walking shoes. We'll meet close to the gate. I'll get everything that we'll need for psychic communication with multiple ghosts."

Multiple ghosts on the third floor?

When I turned to confide my discomfort, Peace was gone—just like she'd done at the food carts. Peace could be a little bit eccentric, but she tapped into the nuances of the universe in a way that I never could—I didn't have anywhere near the talent of Peace.

And I mean, what can go wrong with a little psychic sleuthing in the house?

I'm not convinced that Peace disappears through alien time portals, however. Of course, I never thought stones could talk. And that happened to me in Ireland. And dead O'Malley relatives whispered to me in a cemetery in Belfast. And now a Culloden ghost follows me around Portland but doesn't talk.

Life is complicated.

Later that day at the museum store, I asked Molly to ring up a beaded bracelet that I'd put on hold the night of the gala and had almost forgotten about, but she stopped short of completing the purchase. I'd stashed the bracelet with garnet-colored stones for the next time I needed retail therapy. I needed it now. I was more than a little unnerved that we had numerous ghosts. There had been rumors before, and guests would often ask me if the mansion was haunted. I always told them to remain open to possibilities and to go into the house with an open mind to see for themselves. Little did I really think that I'd been working under a party of ghosts.

"I need to call park rangers," Molly said, looking out the store window toward the parking lot. Her comment shook away my other ruminations, and I looked to where Molly was now pointing.

Peace was standing in the middle of the car lot with an aluminum foil hat on her head. Cars were driving by, honking, giving her the thumbs-up. Usually, Portland is a pretty civil place, accepting to all sorts of weirdness. Peace gave the thumbs-up in return and then raised her arms toward the weak autumn sun in a yoga tree pose, meditating in the middle of the parking lot while wearing an aluminum foil hat. I didn't want Molly to call the park cops, and I didn't want to confess that Peace was a friend of mine. I felt remotely guilty about this, so maybe I needed to work on getting a spine. At any rate, the park rangers were like the police, and I don't like cops. It has to do with my former husband, who was a Portland cop at one time, and he'd caused me plenty of misery. Then I had a terrible thought: *If I conjure ghosts with the microchip, could I suddenly run into my dead husband's ghost?*

I felt sweat trickle down my back at this most disturbing thought. I forced myself to reclaim my calm until I could talk to Peace about it. For now, all I could think to do was distract Molly, so I yanked open the drawer under the counter, pretending to look for a jewelry box. It was a pretty frantic motion, and luckily it grabbed Molly's attention, so when I looked up again, Peace had disappeared.

"The crazy lady is gone," Molly said to me.

I took some glass cleaner from under the counter and wiped the glass surface of the cash-wrap counter.

"All's well that ends well." I didn't know why that Shakespearean phrase popped out of my mouth. As I wiped unseen fingerprints from the counter, I heard the *beep-beep-beep* warning sound of a tourist bus backing up and looked up again. Good. Another distraction. Soon we'd be overrun with silver-haired seniors.

"I'll open the admissions bay," Molly said as she handed me back my Visa card and put my bracelet in a box, then into a Pittock Mansion gift bag, completing the purchase. She logged out of the computer's retail software program so I could log in.

I watched as the over-sixty group exited the vehicle like a line of sugar ants. Knowing that snacks would be flying out of the store soon, I refilled trail mix and mustard pretzels in the basket display, along with bottles of water.

At the end of the day, I finished my reports. The store grossed about six hundred dollars—not a bad profit from books, magnets, postcards, snacks, and bottled water. Our communication method was a walkie-talkie that squawked like a murder of crows; words always came out in a blitz of static.

"Coming in," I alerted Molly, our security protocol. I hustled along the garden pathway to the porte cochère entrance—even as my vision strayed to the pathway that Helen had described she walked down on the night of the gala—and after relocking the mahogany double doors, I made a dash upstairs to the office.

Molly had turned off all the main lights—a feat considering the sixteen thousand square feet of house—along with the gatehouse, another two thousand square feet. In my short time working with Molly, she seemed very efficient. I filled out the deposit slip, we both signed off on it, and I picked up my bag as we both left for the day.

I knew I'd be back later to dig for answers.

Chapter 7
Ghost Hunting

IT'S IMPORTANT TO HAVE THE RIGHT OUTFIT when you go ghost hunting. Plus, I needed some additional retail therapy. A psychotherapist would tell me that shopping provides a substitute for a crazy mother who disappeared from my life when I was very young, or a father who died while I slogged through the formative middle school years, or a psychic aunt who raised me under the microscope of a tiny town on the Oregon coast, or to compensate for a husband who cheated on me, but I didn't bother with therapy sessions. I knew the stories, and I could talk to myself for free.

I dashed into a little boutique on Northwest 23rd Avenue to look for an outfit. It didn't take long to find it: navy-blue leggings with a sweater in a lovely dark gray. I had silver hoop earrings at home, and I'd wear a darkish hat. I found new boots in another boutique on the avenue. A little deeper color of gray, ankle height. *Forget about tennis shoes.* I rocked at fashion.

As I walked home, I relished in the scent of rain-washed air, the fallen leaves of ancient oak trees (planted before the Pittocks' mansion was built—probably when Northwest Portland had been plotted), and I felt the happiest I'd been in a long time. I was past my disastrous marriage, I'd found my Irish family in Ireland, and I had a steady job. Plus, Peace Jones, my slightly eccentric friend, was here to help me.

However, something was nagging at me besides the trauma of finding Allie Campbell-Stone's body in the dumbwaiter—*Oh, and could I run into her ghost?* Something was bugging me about the events of the night of the gala, but it was nebulous, and the harder I tried to figure it out, the more hidden it seemed.

Back at my apartment hallway, I tapped on the door of my neighbor, a musician and part-time student. When he opened the door, I got a wild smell of garlic and stale beer like a hard-party weekend.

"Want an IPA microbrew?" Bryce asked.

I nodded, and he popped the cap off a bottle with his lighter—a skill I'm sure he acquired at college—and handed me a bottle. Then he plopped down on his sagging sofa cushions, grabbed his guitar, and began to strum.

"New song?" I asked.

"Yeah, I'm working on it. It's a breakup song."

He had been on-again, off-again with his girlfriend, a theater major at Lewis & Clark College.

Although we'd been neighbors for a few short months, I had listened to the ups and downs of his rapidly eroding relationship. "Maybe it would be good to be single and figure out what *you* want," I said.

I was aware of the irony that I was giving advice about relationships, and for the briefest of moments, the image of Danny, my Navajo former boyfriend, popped into my mind. But now he was like a ghost from my past. *That relationship is over. Quit looking in the rearview mirror.*

Bryce sang some of the lyrics. "I can't get her out of my mind." *That's the way it works*, I thought.

I drank my beer and finally got to the favor I'd come to ask him. "I'm going to work late tonight and hoped you might be able to give Karma a little company and a quick walk outside."

"Yeah, no problem."

I finished my microbrew and let myself out to the sound of Bryce's guitar. When I got inside my apartment, Karma was napping on the couch.

"Bryce's coming over tonight; he's got girlfriend trouble."

Karma uncurled herself from her warm nest and gave me a wiggly love greeting, plus she was also softening me up for kibble.

After feeding her and giving her a chance to relieve herself outside, I took a quick shower, towel dried my hair, and removed my purchases from the bags. I love the *pop* of taking tags off new clothes from a dopamine-induced retail purchase. Plus, it takes skill not to rip the fabric. It comes with experience.

I've still got the gift.

I got dressed and tucked my hair into a bun after blow-drying it, then adorned my ears with the silver hoops—the perfect jewelry for after-hours sleuthing. One time in Sedona, I'd donned a blonde wig and red lipstick to reveal a crime nest and get my brother out of a pile of trouble.

A little voice in my head said, *Oh, what could happen this time?*

With one last look in the mirror, I tucked my sleuthing flashlight in my coat pocket and silenced my cell phone. I didn't want to take my car, which might draw attention, so I walked up the forested pedestrian edge of Burnside Street and crossed at a blinking yellow light. I found a pocket of peace from the traffic and dashed across the road. On the quieter residential street at the T intersection, I walked by streetlight to the first stop sign and turned right. Like Burnside and many west-side streets in Portland, sidewalks were few and far between.

While walking, I mused. With the population explosion and the rigid urban growth boundary in the Portland real estate market, the economics of supply and demand catered to developers and their high rents. It had also been like that in 1964, when Pittock Mansion was for sale with its forty-six acres; the developers eventually buzzed like vultures over it. If the City of Portland hadn't had the vision to buy the historic house and property, it would have been razed.

At the bottom of the road leading toward the mansion, I stepped around the bolted gate and clicked on my flashlight. When I reached one of the signposts on the road that gave a little tutorial about the mansion—the one about Georgiana Pittock coming on the Oregon Trail—I stopped. I heard an owl hoot in the distance. It's surprising how many mammals and birds of prey live in a dark, urban-forest setting. It was a full moon. I caught movement, and Peace appeared; she'd been hiding behind a hundred-year-old Douglas fir.

"Got everything," Peace said as she tapped the oversized pockets of her cargo pants. It was cold, and I could see her breath. "Here." She broke into a bag of Doritos, took out several, and popped them into her mouth. "Eat some," she said to me.

I looked at the artificially flavored, processed, salty snack—Doritos were not enticing to me, but Peace insisted as she put the bag under my nose.

"The artificial chemicals react with the molecular biology and create a quantum, psychic supercharge. It's like putting fine gasoline into an ultraexpensive automobile."

My fingers turned maize as I grasped several. "When you were at Reed College, when you drank the punch laced with LSD, what was your college major?"

"Mathematical physics, biochemistry, and molecular biology. Triple major. And some nights I played beer pong on the college's nuclear reactor console."

"Ah," I said.

"No one had to evacuate the east side of Portland from beer pong."

I smiled as I faced the dark silhouette of the gate lodge in front of us. "That's where the Scottish caretaker lived," I said, pointing with my Doritos-stained fingers at the haunted-looking building. "Henry and Georgiana didn't have many servants in 1914. There was a cook and a few house servants who lived on the third floor of the mansion next to Henry's study. The chauffeur lived with his wife in the small apartment above the three-bay garage. I was sent to Scotland to get possessions that were part of the Skene family. Mr. Skene, the groundskeeper, lived there, in the gate lodge with his wife and daughter."

"Any ghosts in the gate lodge?"

I shrugged since I hadn't picked up on the spirits in the mansion. "Actually, Molly Murphy, a colleague, confessed to me that she gets chills in the gate lodge—before she scurries out when it's her turn to close it. But she's supposed to check all floors and windows, everything."

"What about you?" she asked.

"I about peed in my pants when I heard music in there—until I realized they'd hooked the gramophone to a motion detector in the parlor." I blushed. "I haven't told anyone that before."

"Any security personnel in the big house?" Peace crunched another Dorito and looked toward the mansion.

"Only an alarm. I'll deactivate it."

We'd reached the porte cochère entrance, and once inside, I tapped the alarm pad with the code to disarm it.

"We better use the flashlight," I said as I removed it from my pocket. "Otherwise someone might report lights on in the house..."

Before I finished, Peace had raced upstairs. "I'm sensing something up here," she said, calling over the banister and then running up another flight. I ran to catch up to her, up the grand white-marble staircase to the second floor, then through the door with the sign that read *Staff Only*. Up the narrow, spiraled servant stairs, Peace dashed into Henry's study with me right behind her. I'd tapped into something, too, because the chip had grown extra hot under my skin.

Astoundingly, in front of us was Henry Pittock's ghost. He stood five feet tall in his boots, with a fashionable white beard coiffed into a point, but he wasn't completely solid—I could see the window casements through him, and vintage furniture appeared in the room. Pittock was holding a photograph as he turned to the wall of built-in mahogany storage, each compartment with its own key. It was where staff and volunteers stored and locked their personal items.

What happened next stirred me with anxiety because Pittock began *fading*. And this was before I could think to communicate with him about the mansion or any of his family members who were residing in the house as ghosts. Frustrated, I noticed that the tacky office furniture that I used every day now surrounded me, instead of the vintage pieces that had surrounded Henry moments before.

Peace put her hand on my shoulder. "Hate to interrupt, but someone's coming."

That's when I heard the elevator grind to a stop and someone fumbling to release the door catch on the Otis.

"We have to hide!" I mouthed the words, and my feet flew, Peace close behind me. There was the storage room. We hustled into it and flattened ourselves against the wall, then lowered ourselves to hide behind the curator's artifacts in the very dark room. I mostly held my breath until we finally heard the elevator door close and the grinding of the gears going down, signaling the departure of the party crasher.

Who is in the mansion at this time of night?

"That was close," Peace said, though she now felt safe enough to crunch another Dorito. "Any idea who busted up our ghost party?" she added.

"No. But a ghost wouldn't use a noisy elevator to get upstairs."

I'd grown aches and pains from the cloistered closet. I finally whispered to Peace. "I think the coast is clear. Are you getting any sixth-sense feelings?"

She ate another Dorito, licked her finger, and held it up in the air. "All the spirits and living intruders have temporarily vanished."

"Let's get out of here."

I turned on the mansion's alarm system as we left through the porte cochère doors. We'd decided to debrief at a Pearl District bar since it was too late for any retail outings.

Chapter 8
At the Bar

FUNERALS, DEATH, BREAKUPS, AND GHOST encounters lead me to alcohol. I'd ordered whisky, even though I usually preferred wine. But tonight, I had a distinct craving for the taste of smoke-infused aged Scotch. Peace tossed back a shot and put her finger in the air to signal the bartender for another.

I felt it was urgent to confront Peace with my misgivings. "Now that I can see ghosts, or conjure them, I'm worried that my former husband might come back and haunt me. Is that possible?"

Peace laughed. "Highly unlikely. Your microchip is a boost for spirits that want to be with you. Your Scottish ghost is playing coy because he likes you. In another time, you'd probably have some kind of relationship with him. But your husband is finished with you. You've told me that, and I don't think you'd allow him to come back."

I audibly sighed. *Thank goodness.* Something still troubled me, but I couldn't quite make a clear thought about it. "So, I have some control over who appears to me?"

"Got it," she said, tossing back the shot of Scotch.

I felt relieved by her words. I didn't want to see my two-timing crap-ass dead husband again, and I tossed back my shot.

"Tell me what you remember about the ghost—Mr. Pittock—the original owner of the house," Peace asked.

"It all happened so quickly," I said. "But he was staring at a photograph or something like it, and he seemed sad, or emotionally ill."

Now I'm psychoanalyzing ghosts.

"Who do you think interrupted us?"

I nervously fiddled with the amulet in my pocket that Trinity had given me. "It could have been Jonathan Applegate, or another board member. It could have been Anthony Baker, the former curator, if he still has a key. As far as I know, he was fired. I really don't know for sure, but I've also heard rumors about a tunnel entrance."

Peace sighed. "And the person in the house tonight might be tipped off that we were there because the alarm was off while we were inside. They didn't reset it. Either they didn't know how to do it, or were concerned the code wouldn't work anymore, or it was someone who knew but didn't want to change the way it was found."

"I'm a little worried, but it could be an easy mistake—that I forgot to arm it earlier in the evening, when I left."

"Have you talked to your former boss about his dismissal?"

Now that was a solid idea. "I should do that. I've been thinking about him. I really don't know why he was let go, or was fired, or quit. It all happened so quickly, and then I was in Scotland."

"And I think we should visit the house again, after hours, and try to find a tunnel entrance," Peace suggested.

"Agreed."

Peace's finger went up to order a third round of shots.

Later, everything about that night made sleep difficult. When the alarm clock rang and I hadn't slept much, what seemed even worse was that when I had dozed, I dreamed about Danny, my Navajo ex-boyfriend, holding me in his arms, kissing my neck.

For the love of all that is holy, this has got to stop.

As I opened one eye, I spied Mac resting on the floor next to me. He'd been watching me as Karma slept next to him. "I've got to get ready for work, Mac." Throwing my legs out of bed, I worked my way around a sleeping Labrador and a lustful Highland ghost.

Drinking my coffee while I walked Karma, I was nursing a blinding hangover headache. Thankfully, Mac disappeared when we got back to the apartment, so I didn't have to deal with him while I got ready. After my shower, I used extra makeup to compensate for my lack of shut-eye and my hangover, and I still made it to work fifteen minutes early. Entering the porte cochère doors, I greeted Molly, who was hanging her coat in the cloakroom. I attempted to present a calm, professional demeanor. I inhaled deeply and repeated the mantra: *All is well.*

I also rehearsed damage control with possible excuses if my presence in the mansion last night was called out. I decided to say that I'd forgotten something—like my phone. It seemed like an excellent plan. But when I got upstairs to my office, I had another surprise waiting for me.

"I'm adding another responsibility," Jonathan Applegate said. He was sitting in my work chair. "You'll be hosting Saturday's Behind the Scenes Tour."

Me?

Now this was kind of exciting since it was hugely popular and I'd be able to take small groups of tourists into the underbelly of the mansion.

Mr. Applegate handed me a large file. "Here's the information."

And just like that, he left. I mentally included him as a suspect, like everyone else at the mansion the night Allie Campbell-Stone died.

The architect Edward Foulkes had been a native Oregonian. He'd studied at Stanford and the Massachusetts Institute of Technology. It took him five years from planning to construction to finish the mansion. My head was filled with details about the Washington State Tenino sandstone, crafted on-site for the exterior of the mansion, along with the Italian Tavernelle buff marble used in the pillars, pilasters, and doorways of the stairways. The white marble on the floors was from California. I religiously jotted down the facts. When I finally came up for air, I realized I'd been in that zone where time appears to stop. I had dozens of note cards filled with Pittock Mansion behind-the-scenes material. Molly walked in, and I realized the day was over.

"You got the tour duty," she said as she glanced at my notes. "I get nervous talking in front of groups."

"I like it," I said, clearly enjoying my new responsibility.

Cashing out the tills for admissions and the museum store went like clockwork. We left the mansion together, another suggested protocol, although not always followed.

In my car, I headed down the hill toward my apartment, but the traffic on Burnside Street slowed to a crawl, so when I got the Zupan's Markets driveway, I pulled into the high-end grocery store to peruse the ready-to-eat dinners while the traffic thinned. I could have walked back to my place faster than driving.

Even though I understood about supply and demand and gentrification, the population explosion in the city—especially the inner northwest and the southeast sides of Portland—made me sad. I wondered what the original landowners—the Ladd, Pittock, and Benson families—would think about Portland with the big developers changing the landscape.

I once more nudged into the merging traffic on Burnside Street and finally arrived at my apartment with my Zupan's chicken rice bowl with plum sauce, and it was still warm.

I'd decided to review my notes—the French-styled music room, the English-crafted library, the Craftsman-styled dining room, and the circular Turkish smoking room, along with the inlaid wood floors, which had not been damaged by the Columbus Day Storm of 1962, although other rooms had suffered from rainwater leaks.

"Remember, 1962 for the storm. The mansion was purchased by the City in 19—"

My memorization was interrupted by the doorbell. I peered through the peephole like a pirate through a looking glass. Bryce's big eyeball looked back at me. "Developers got us," my neighbor hollered as I opened the door. "Thirty-day eviction notice," he said as he waved the legal notice. "What are we going to do?"

A thirty-day no-fault eviction notice. Portland's liberal and weird city had congealed into an overcrowded urban development—with rental properties converted into high-scale, very expensive condominiums.

I had another move in my future.

I'd bought a fall-colored scarf at the museum store—plaid with a blue background with orange and mustard tones and a touch of maroon (really, the colors worked)—and now added it to my white shirt and black slacks. I put on my ankle boots, black, with the zipper and a little bit of heel that screamed, *I'm in charge, and I know what I'm talking about.* I decided to add my silver earrings and a bangle of a silver bracelet, and I had *sass* written all over me. Besides the joy of retail therapy, the right clothes give you confidence.

Arriving early on Saturday, I unlocked and disarmed the admissions bay and easily found the file for the Behind the Scenes guests. Orders for the event came through admissions, where the purchase was applied to a credit card. In other words, they were prepaid.

Some areas were off-limits to all guests except tour groups, and because of fire regulations, only small groups were allowed for tours. We'd have four groups throughout the day, and each tour was under an hour. The credit card receipts included the notes of the number in the party, the amount paid, along with the last name of the group. We kept an Excel sheet with more information, so I logged on to the computer and printed out a copy to the admissions desk printer, where we also had storage for extra-large backpacks and strollers. Not allowed: selfie sticks. The bane of museums.

I logged off the computer, rekeyed the alarm, and locked the admissions door. Approaching the mansion, a couple was already milling at the entrance. Over the next fifteen minutes, the remainder of the tour arrived—mostly seniors.

I patted the note cards in my pocket next to my Cajun amulet from Trinity and handed out the required lanyards to guests. Introducing myself first, we started the tour at the gate lodge. Leading the way, I explained that the road had been changed and how the Pittocks' 1912 Pierce-Arrow would have made its way to the porte cochère entrance, then continued around the road with the stunning view of Mount Hood on a clear day, toward the gate lodge, and on down the road that was now permanently closed to vehicles.

We entered through the main door of the caretaker's lodge. "The gate lodge includes some original furnishings," I said as I pushed the buttons to turn on the electric lights. "The mantel clock is original from the Skene family, a Scottish couple who lived here with their daughter from approximately 1918 until the mid-1950s. The chauffeur and his wife occupied the gate lodge for the first four years, from 1914 until 1918, until they moved to the apartment over the three-bay garage."

Taking a deep breath, I gathered everyone around the new display case that held the antiquities I'd been sent to Inverness to retrieve.

"Here are two new items that we recently added to the museum collection." The guests viewed the new display of the quaich—I explained the use and history of the goodwill drinking cup—and the dueling pistols with the accessories. "Be sure to also check out the Skene family treasures on the wall." In a case was a tartan tie in muted red tones along with some other small family artifacts.

All in all, the new acquisitions round out the gate lodge experience.

By the time we left the lodge, it was turning out to be a fair-weather day. Pointing up to the parking lot where Peace had assumed her alien yoga pose days ago, I explained that greenhouses had once stood there, but that the Columbus Day Storm of 1962 had left them in disrepair and the City had removed them when they purchased the mansion and the forty-six acres of property in 1964 for $225,000.

Finished with the gatehouse, I led the group to the next phase of the tour. We entered the porte cochère entrance of the mansion, where a volunteer was stationed at the greeting podium. I took my group around her to the main lobby and spoke about expensive marble, the universal symbols and motifs in the plaster friezes, the eucalyptus curved-wood railing of the staircase, the hidden drains for the inside planter boxes, the brass outlets for the 1914 central vacuum, and the family members who originally lived in the house. I explained that Henry and Georgiana Pittock had been elderly when they moved in, and she'd had a mild stroke beforehand, so Henry included the Otis elevator as part of the original construction.

One elderly man stood in the outer circle and appeared to be a single in a world of tourist couples. Since he'd positioned himself at the fringe of the group, I hadn't really noticed him before.

I asked, "Any questions so far?"

"Where's the food storage?" the man asked.

Well, that's an interesting question.

"After we pass through the breakfast room, you'll see the storage room on your right," I said.

Leading the way, I stopped in the breakfast nook that looked out toward the garden and the admissions office. Dark, exotic-floral wallpaper colored the walls in this room, contrasting with the light playing through the window. Plum-colored flowers popped from the walls, entangled with green ferns and vines. "This was the gathering spot for the family, and it is where Henry Pittock ate grapefruit everyday—imported. Note the Depression glass in the table setting. Oh, and there are souvenir earrings in the museum store with the wallpaper motif." *Note to self: Wear the jewelry from the store to increase sales!*

I turned to exit through the hallway door, passing the refrigerator room so everyone in the group could peer through the doorway of this roped-off room.

"Please note the full-wall refrigeration system—a marvel for the time. The outside walls were designed with extra thickness when the house was built, to assist with the cooling." Now before turning into the kitchen, I nodded toward the pantry. "Here's the food storage." The shelves held canned goods.

"For the staff and a family of ten? That's too small for that many people." This comment was from the same man.

All eyes turned toward me.

"Streets were unpredictable and unreliable," he said.

"And?"

"There's underground storage, a tunnel, like a priest's hole," he insisted.

A shiver ran over me, like someone stepped on Aunt Thelma's grave. "That's an interesting theory," I said. "Now, we need to keep moving."

We descended to the bottom floor, where we entered the inner back rooms of the mansion, only accessible by tour or to staff, where I showed the group the infrastructure of the house. After we got through the electrical panels—still with the original fuses—we examined the elevator room on the same floor. "The Otis Elevator Company continues to service and maintain the elevator for the mansion."

We backed out of the small room and in single file made our way down the hallway toward the west side of the building and Henry's vault. An overhead lightbulb was all the lighting for the small room, and I noted that the walls appeared to be solid concrete, except for wooden shelves that held some of the museum store's overstock.

Mac appeared to me, and the temperature in Henry's vault was about twenty-five degrees cooler than usual, but no one seemed to suspect that it was because a ghost had dropped in.

"Henry Pittock invested in the stock market and kept his paper stocks and bonds in here. It is located under the porte cochère entrance and believed to be the most fireproof room in the mansion." I held up a laminated article from the *Oregonian* about when the house had been under construction and passed it around.

Finishing the tour, I led the guests to the main level of the house and answered any last questions. When it was over, Mac clapped.

It was then that I decided what I'd have to do next. I'd come back to the mansion in the dead of night and tap around for a tunnel. I'd go over every inch of the house, and sleuth around outside too, looking for an entrance. If it was there, I was determined to find it.

Chapter 9
A Change in the Wind

LIFE IS COMPLICATED. AND MESSY. *And mostly unpredictable.*

When I'm in a mental review like this, I like to flip things toward the positive. This technique came from my new age Aunt Thelma. My paternal side was Catholic, but I've avoided the Catholic guilt, thanks to my mixed-religion family.

New age Catholicism.

I had the day off. *And how to unwind after finding a body and dealing with ghost encounters?*

I stopped to stock up on some of the essential hard spirits, available in Oregon only from licensed liquor stores. The history is that after Prohibition, the state government wanted control, so it formed the OLCC—Oregon Liquor Control Commission—and to this day it regulates the distribution and sale. I was standing at the counter in front of the salesperson when I got my first wave of *I don't feel well.* Like someone came up from behind me and hit me over the head.

Maybe it's a bad oyster. I'd stopped for some shooters at Jake's Grill, one of the old Portland eating establishments. Eating oysters is like gulping down seawater; it reminds me of the lazy days of summer living.

My stomach was still unsettled when I got home, so I rummaged through the cupboard for some loose-leaf tea. I found Aunt Thelma's tea set—a Belleek teapot with creamer and sugar and four cups and saucers—and went about heating water for a cup of oolong.

Aunt Thelma was the best tea-leaf reader in the family. Nora, my Irish relative on the remote Beara Peninsula in County Cork, Ireland, was almost as good. Nora could see the magic of the fairy lights in the distant cliffs from her house, but my prominent psychic gift was psychometry, the feeling of a person from an object.

The tea water was boiling; the kettle sung on the burner like a monk chanting. *A perfect note*, I thought. Grabbing a quilt from my bed, I wrapped it around me and smelled lavender. That was Aunt Thelma's favorite aromatic scent, and it felt like she'd joined me at the kitchen table for a cup. *Will Aunt Thelma appear to me?* Peace's words trickled through me about the chip and my free will. *No, Aunt Thelma and I are at peace. She's always with me.*

I began the tea-reading ritual: I warmed the Irish china pot with some of the boiling water, poured the remainder of the hot water into it, and pinched the loose tea into the teapot. For a one-person reading, I used about a teaspoon of the oolong tea, letting the tea steep. I started to relax even more, happy to be in the present, and Karma plopped at my feet.

All is well. All is well. All is well.

I sipped the tea and thought about the question to ask.

Who murdered Allie Campbell-Stone?

I heard Karma's rhythmic breathing as she fell into a deep sleep, and I watched as she twitched, chasing imaginary rabbits.

I sipped my tea until I was down to the last teaspoon of liquid. Then I took the teacup in my left hand and swirled it three times counterclockwise before I flipped the cup upside down and let the remaining liquid drip into the saucer. When I examined the leaves in the cup, I focused my thoughts on the question I'd intentioned.

The first place I looked was left of the cup handle, the traditional reading in a counterclockwise pattern. The rim and upper lip of the cup represent the most immediate future, the middle section further in time, and the lower level is the far future.

Trust your intuition.

My cup lip had two tea blots. One looked like a snake, an omen for a difficult time in my career. *That's the truth.* The second was a chair—an indicator that I'd soon have something new in my career. *Well, that is interesting.* Peering into the middle section, I detected the shape of a square, symbolizing my progress in solving the murder would be blocked. There was also a mountain, meaning that I would be faced with frustrating and almost insurmountable odds. *I'll take it one step at a time to figure it out.* In the lower level, I spied a cloud and a bell, meaning there were things that I'd overlooked and I needed to concentrate. I was not to make assumptions about anything. And finally, a shark, meaning a predator was out there, watching and waiting for me.

I stifled a shiver and looked for some paper to write down my tasseomancy—tea-reading—details. I found a partially used journal inserted in the middle of my aunt's favorite cookbook. Aunt Thelma had enjoyed a collection of books about crystals and tea readings, and other new age topics. Many books had gone with her to the assisted living center, but she'd mailed some to me when I was struggling with my psychic identity and a murder in Sedona.

When I was in middle and high school, Aunt Thelma would tuck away a daily meditation and her tea reading for me before I'd go off to school for the day. In her neat script, she'd predict the outcome of a test or the possibility of romance. I didn't accept her ways back then because I didn't want to be different, but with chilling clarity, I now read her black-ink script on the journal page and could see the utter turmoil in my life she'd predicted at the time—I broke up with a boyfriend and hurtled into the next mistake, my marriage doomed to fail.

I flipped to a fresh page to write the impressions of my newest reading, thinking this pesky ghost business was beyond anything I remembered with Aunt Thelma. After I recorded my thoughts, I went to where I'd kept the remainder of my aunt's books. Riffling through the spines—looking for something to intuitively jump out—I took an unusual one from her collection of new age titles. It was about the early years of Portland's history.

I don't recall this book in her collection. But it found me, manifested in some way by my late aunt, kismet.

Mac appeared as I started reading about the mayhem that had filled the early years in Portland. He took out his dirk and began to sharpen it in a slow, rhythmic fashion, like he was getting ready for battle. Since Mac didn't talk, most of our communication was through expressions and gestures. Now, I ignored him and got back to the task at hand—reading about Portland's past might lead me to answers about today and maybe, if I was lucky, a possible reason for Allie Campbell-Stone's murder.

What I read in the book about the Pittock family were details I already knew—that Henry Pittock died in 1919 of grippe. The Spanish flu pandemic raged from 1918 through 1920, and he lost his beloved wife, Georgiana, the year before. The senior Pittocks hadn't lived in the house for more than a few years before they passed. One grandchild continued to live at the estate until the 1950s, when he moved out and put it up for sale. Before long, it was a forlorn house in need of an owner. None appeared until the City of Portland purchased it and the forty-six acres of property after the Columbus Day Storm of 1962 had wreaked havoc on the abandoned mansion. For years after, the roof leaked rainwater where trees had fallen and cracked the clay roof tiles.

About the time that the mansion was completed, 1914, Prohibition arrived early in Oregon, and Portland's trade links with Seattle and Vancouver, British Columbia, allowed illegal alcohol to be supplied to the speakeasies. And many Portland cops, and the mayor, were on the take back then. This didn't surprise me. I knew a little bit about early Portland and its dabbling into illegal spirits. Actually, moonshine was plentiful in Portland in those early years. There were forested areas, places to hide, and dirty cops who could be bribed. An ocean and a railway to move the product. It was a natural place to brew spirits in those early days.

As the evening twilight took over, I stopped reading. My stomach felt better than it had earlier. Setting aside the book, I rubbed my eyes and decided to try to take a nap. But as I worked for some shut-eye, I still puzzled over the questions: What was to be gained by Allie Campbell-Stone's murder? And why had it happened at Pittock Mansion?

There had to be some reason, and most likely the explanation was somewhere in the relationships with the others at the mansion that night.

Mac replaced his now-very-pointy dirk into its leather case and disappeared.

As I started to slip off to sleep, I remembered that I'd planned to visit Anthony Baker, but my unsettled stomach had temporarily postponed it.

It would turn out to be an unfortunate delay.

Chapter 10

Nina

"I've been talking to Nina," Peace said as she slipped into the booth for dinner at the Old Town Pizza parlor in a semi-rough section of Portland's Old Town Chinatown. Before it became a pizza place, the building had been the historic Merchant Hotel. It rested on top of the infamous Shanghai Tunnels of Portland, the notorious markers for Portland's dark past of smuggling, rum-running, and human trafficking. Who would know that funky, artistic Portland had such a traumatic history?

I blamed it all on the gray, rainy, endless days of wet.

Tunnels. I didn't like mine shafts, or tunnels, or being kidnapped. I'd had a brush with all three, and I couldn't shake the feeling that some tunnels were hiding up at the mansion's estate grounds.

The pizza came, and I took up a large slice of vegetarian.

When I took one bite of the rich cheese, my taste buds celebrated the ooze of the pizza, an after-work treat. There were the gooey textures, the crunch of the crust, and the flavors of onions, green bell peppers, and mushrooms that exploded in a marriage in my mouth—followed by the honeymoon taste of the wash of a cold Pacific Northwest microbrew.

Orgasmic.

By the second slice, I was talking about my tea-leaf reading. I interjected that I still needed to find a new place to live. "Maybe I'll call my uncle." I grabbed an unheard-of third slice of pie. I didn't have much time to look for a new place to live. "It's a tidal wave of thirty-day no-cause eviction notices in Portland."

"No luck?" Peace asked.

I'd gone as far as looking on Craigslist and Zillow. "Things are rough out there. Plus, I have a large dog, so that limits the possibilities." I was discouraged, but I hadn't given up yet. I always had Uncle Callaghan's couch to fall back on, and I could move back to my beach house in Manzanita—except that I didn't have a job at the beach, it was too far to commute, and it wouldn't take long for me to blast through my savings.

Peace and I tossed around some ideas, but the bottom line was that I needed time to look and I didn't have much of that. She was living temporarily with a professor from Reed College until she headed back to Sedona.

When the server brought the check to the table, I was feeling pretty good about the evening—heavy on the carbohydrate load, a little buzz from the beer, but a warm feeling with a friend who didn't judge me as crazy. When I looked at the check, the name of our server, Jessica, stood out, but then I recalled that Peace had said she'd spoken to Nina, and I realized I'd made an *assumption* it was our server.

I furrowed my eyebrows. "Who's Nina? You said you were talking to her when you sat down in the booth."

"She's over there." Peace pointed in the direction of the pizza oven. Standing there was a pretty young girl, dressed in a long black dress, maybe eighteen years old, and faded.

"Nina's a ghost?"

"And she's got something to show us." Peace pointed under the table. "She knows the tunnels. She came over and communicated with me before you got here."

I'd read about the floorboards that opened to the dark Portland tunnels, where drunken loggers and cowboys, drugged, fell through a trapdoor when an accomplice bartender pulled a special lever when the time was ripe. Waking up, the unsuspecting were on a ship, forced to serve out their time at sea, shanghaied.

I looked at the man throwing the pizza dough. He apparently couldn't see Nina as she playfully interfered with his job, the dough almost falling to the floor.

She stopped messing with the cute pizza maker and waved to me. I gulped air.

Peace and I left money for the pizza with a tip and followed Nina through the arch of a doorway toward the back of the restaurant. Peace put her hand on my shoulder as I cautiously turned the doorknob of the door Nina had walked through, and it yielded. Looking around the main dining area, I saw the staff was busy, and before anyone could tell us this area was off limits, we were inside a corridor, with a floor of packed earth.

"I've read about these tunnels; all lead to the river. When a captain needed men, he would put the word out, and loggers and cowboys were shanghaied," I said as I felt the hairs on my neck in full salute.

Nina pointed toward a set of stairs and abruptly disappeared.

"Wait. I have questions!" My voice echoed in the empty tunnel. Apparently, Nina had other plans. "Nina's not one for sticking around," I said to Peace.

"Ghosts can be kind of picky that way."

"Maybe we should check out where she pointed before she disappeared."

Walking over to the spot, I saw a playbill and quickly recognized it as one from the gala. I'd made sure I handed one to all the guests that night.

"What do you think?" I asked.

"I think you should tell me everything you remember about that night. Start from the afternoon when you were getting prepared."

I recounted to Peace what I remembered: "I helped select the wine for the theater and dinner this year—Crime and Dine. The theater was a new addition to the venue, and I was determined to make it a great show and evening. I'd made my way through the mansion's wine cellar earlier to find our overstock vintage metal wine corkscrews but couldn't locate any. Mr. Baker wanted to display some of the new stock from the museum store with the wine. I had to go out to the store to rummage through cabinets there, looking through all the mismatched boxes."

"Tell me what else you recall," Peace encouraged.

"I was in the store, and you know about me and jewelry. I was searching for the corkscrews, but I just had to stop and look at some of the bracelets. I found this piece that I fell in love with, so I tucked it inside the top drawer of the cash wrap and put my name on it to hold."

"Then what happened?"

"I walked back to the mansion, entered through the porte cochère entrance, and went up to the staff-only door to the third-floor office when all of a sudden, a powerful gust of wind blew into the room. The windows shook, and papers shuffled in front of me like a dealer cutting cards in Vegas." I lowered my voice. "I haven't told anyone about it, and I didn't see a ghost, but it felt like something was present. Then I put the corkscrews on Mr. Baker's desk and went to change for the evening. I had a brilliant vintage dress to wear that I'd found shopping at a boutique on Clinton Street, and it fit like a glove. Afterward, I went to see the actors. I'd convinced Curator Baker to stage the play in the library since it was the Agatha Christie play *The Mousetrap*. So when I heard the scream, I had almost everyone in the library except for four of the guests: the doctor, Allie Campbell-Stone, the developer, and the developer's wife."

After listening to the minutiae of what led up to the gala, Peace glared at the black-gray walls of the tunnel, the bowels of Old Town Portland.

"Four guests hadn't made it to the library when you heard the scream: the doctor, Allie Campbell-Stone, the developer, and his wife."

"Yes, that's what I remember."

"Then what did you do?"

"I called my Uncle Callaghan from the broom closet. After that, I went into the bathroom, and the developer's wife came in. For a second, I thought she was going to say something to me, but she went into a stall. She'd been crying, I think. I pinched my checks to look perky since I was pale after finding the body and then went out to triage the evening."

Peace gingerly handed me the playbill, using a napkin as a makeshift glove. "See what your friends at the coast, with the lab connections, can do with this." I knew she was talking about Trinity and Sheriff Griffin. I'd ask them for the favor, but right now, it felt like I was living a game of Clue.

Nina didn't reappear, so we exited the same way we'd come, past the overworked kitchen crew and pizza crust-throwing man, and out the exit to the cold Portland night. A light mist was in the air, giving the streetlights a haze that made it feel more like nineteenth-century Scotland than Portland, Oregon.

"Did that trip to the tunnels help?" I asked, unsure that our quick adventure in the underbelly of Portland had served a purpose at all.

"It was an introduction. There's no telling what Nina knows."

Peace was right. I kicked some loose gravel with my toe and slipped the playbill into my bag.

Chapter 11

Communication from the Grave

THE NEXT DAY AT WORK was pleasant, but as I was headed on the path toward my car at the end of the day, while passing by the three-bay garage, I heard a strange sound. It was coming from the admissions bay—a buzzing, like something electrical. Molly had left a little bit early for a dental appointment, so I was alone to investigate. I got to the side door of the admissions bay and unlocked it and disarmed the alarm.

It was quiet again, so I sat down, waiting.

There it is again.

The buzzing sound was coming from the upstairs.

I climbed the steps to the abandoned second-floor apartment. Expecting the apartment door to be the locked, I was surprised that it was open. I never had a reason to go to the apartment before, so I had no idea what to expect inside. It was rumored that it had been years since anyone lived there. The lights didn't work when I tried the switch, so I used my cell phone to illuminate the entry. All I saw were dust and cobwebs, sheet-covered furniture, and stacks of old *Oregonian* newspapers from the 1960s.

A firetrap, for sure. Maybe it had always been like this. But what about the noise?

None of my psychic warnings went off. As I backed out of the apartment, I heard the ring of a phone. But it wasn't the business phone in the admissions bay—it was the vintage wall phone from 1914, the one that Mr. Pittock would have used to call the chauffeur to request the 1912 Pierce-Arrow be driven to the porte cochère entrance to pick up Mrs. Pittock for a ride downtown to visit her friends. Curator Baker had told me that the original phone system didn't work and the City wasn't going to fix it.

Picking up the receiver, I said, "Hello?"

There was static, and then the line went dead.

Am I getting a phone call from the dead?

I briefly felt tingles, like someone walked over Aunt Thelma's grave.

By the time I got to my car, the third-floor balcony, Henry Pittock's terrace, had a trace covering of snow. It was beginning to look like the winter postcard we sold in the museum store. At that moment, I acknowledged that it was a really fine old house with its quirks and noises, even restless ghosts.

At home, I poured some wine, rinsed some lettuce and tore it into bite-sized pieces for a green salad, and chopped a cucumber and half of a green pepper and sprinkled both on top of the torn-lettuce salad. I had a bottle of ranch dressing that would pair well. I also tossed pasta into boiling water and then drained it and made a quick Alfredo sauce of melted butter, half-and-half, salt, pepper, and Parmesan cheese. *Easy peasy.*

After that, I emailed the website company that managed the

mansion's technology about posting the closure for tomorrow due to the weather. A few snowflakes shut Portland down, and snow in the West Hills brought my job and the house to a standstill.

Peace arrived, and I poured her a glass of pinot gris. She glanced around my apartment and asked, "Where is that handsome Highlander?"

"I don't know. He comes and goes like a teenager in love. I think he's found love and is dating our Portland tunnel ghost, Nina."

Peace smiled at the news. "Well, speaking about relationships, there's something to tell you. Your former Sedona boyfriend, Danny, walked into my Arizona shop, like he knew I was coming to Portland, and brought you up. He asked me to give you the message that he wished things could have turned out differently for the two of you."

I didn't miss a beat, my green-eyed jealousy active. "Did he talk about that other girlfriend of his, that vixen, Chavez?"

"Well, no. And personally, I like talking to aliens better than getting in the middle of relationships. And besides, I'm sure you haven't joined a convent since you left Sedona."

I refilled my wineglass and took a gulp. It's hard when someone holds up the mirror of truth for you to get a good look at yourself.

I changed the subject because I just didn't want to hear any more about it.

The next day was a snow day, so I bundled for the cold, took Karma for a romp in the park to play, brought her back to the apartment for a doggie nap, and then went to Old Town Pizza, which was open, for my lunch. I also wanted to see if I could meet with Nina again. When I arrived at the restaurant, it wasn't crowded. I ordered a small pie and a Diet Coke and seated myself in a booth with a brick backdrop. It was uneventful until I was about ready to leave and I felt a presence across from me in the booth. I lifted my eyes and watched Nina manifest. When she'd formed into a ghost, she smiled, and I saw slightly crooked white teeth. A haunting smile. The booth grew cold around me, but my microchip was hot.

Nina made a gesture like she needed to write. I rummaged in my bag until I found a pen. She took it up in her hand, and I passed over a napkin.

Then, poof, she disappeared before she wrote anything.

Dang.

Then I saw why she'd departed. The server was staring at the pen and the napkin, face as white as parchment.

"Did you see that pen move by itself?" she asked.

I took it to mean that she saw Nina drawing, but she didn't see Nina the ghost. Sometimes, it's best to let the other person talk.

"I've seen this happen before in here," she said. "I almost quit the first time it happened, but I needed my job. But you don't seem surprised."

"I work at Pittock Mansion, and we have some crazy stories. Guests ask me all the time if it's haunted."

She nodded. "That mansion has a reputation, and not to take anything away from your ghosts up on the hill, but this place is dizzying with crazy stuff. Have you heard about Nina?"

Oh, this is getting good. "Tell me," I encouraged.

She pointed to the brick-wall backdrop of the booth. "That was an elevator shaft in its former life. This building was first a hotel, and it offered certain services, if you know what I mean. You're in Nina's booth right now. It gets the most haunted action." She gestured again to the rustic red-clay brick stones. "The old elevator shaft is where Nina was found dead."

Now she really had my attention.

"Nina was young. I don't know what happened to her family, but she was left to her own devices to survive, so she was a prostitute," the server said. "Then, along came the Holy Rollers who wanted to clean up Portland. Somehow, they got to Nina and convinced her to name the people who were involved in the sex trafficking—even promised to keep her safe."

I rolled my eyes. I know things don't go well for whistle-blowers—in government, education, business, or religion, it doesn't matter. If it's an organization and money or someone in power is threatened—well, the truth tellers get the ax, metaphorically or literally.

So, the holy missionaries were responsible for Nina's death.

"She was found, dead, at the bottom of the elevator shaft. Someone pushed her—they never found who did it."

My server stifled a shiver. What she couldn't see was that Nina was next to her, trying to console her.

I took TriMet, the Portland bus system, to get to the east side of the river, where Anthony Baker's house was. For orientation, Portland is split in the directions of the compass by the Willamette River, which divides the east and west sides of Portland, and Burnside Street, which separates the north and south sides of the city.

Mr. Baker lived on Southeast Division Street. The neighborhood had been gentrified from a working-class district with hardware stores and auto shops to a Portland hipster destination. There wasn't a parking place available on the street, so I was glad that I'd used public transportation.

My former boss's address was an old-style Portland Craftsman house that had been converted into two apartments. The first thing

I noticed was that Mr. Baker's mailbox was filled with mail. Thinking that a bit odd, I knocked and waited. There was no answer, so I rang the bell.

No response. A gray cat, feral looking, came up the steps, curious. He rubbed his body around my legs. All I got in return was a *meow* before he darted off.

Looking around, I saw there were garbage cans on the side of the house, a driveway where I saw Mr. Baker's car parked, and a window to the house next to the driveway. Now more than curious, I turned the glass-recycling bin over and used it as a footstep to prop myself on the larger plastic bin usually used for comingled recycling. It was precarious, so I grabbed the ledge with peeling pea-green paint and stood to peer inside.

I could see, not surprisingly, that Mr. Baker went for vintage furniture. I stopped my voyeurism when I saw a boot on the floor, attached to a prostrate body.

I've never smoked a cigarette, but I would have if I had one while I waited for the emergency responders, my hands shaking from the shock. The fire truck got there first and then the EMTs, followed by the Portland cops. That's when I overheard the status called in as a DRT—dead right there. It's a term I'd heard Trinity and Sheriff Griffin use. I was told to wait after giving my statement to the first cop on the scene, so I was standing on the sidewalk, trying to stay out of the way, when I called Uncle Callaghan. He didn't pick up, so I left a very brief description about what I'd discovered.

That's when a lab cop walked over to me. I recognized him as the one who had been at the mansion after the murder of Allie Campbell-Stone.

"Yeah," I said before he talked, in a preemptive strategy on my part. "I met you at the Pittock Mansion the night of the gala. I work there, and that man in the house"—I gestured toward it—"was my former boss."

"You were the theater person at the event."

"Right. And I only stood on the recycle bins today because I could see the mail piled up, and I wanted to see if he was okay because I hadn't heard from him."

He jotted it all down, even though I'd told the same thing to the first cop, and then he handed me his business card. "I'm usually at Kells in the evening. If you'd like to get together to talk, or if you think of anything else that you remember, or if you want to have a drink with me, I'm there most evenings."

"So, I'm free to go?"

"Yes."

The last time I got involved with a cop was in Sedona, and I didn't plan on making that kind of mistake again. Lucky for me, this one was called back to the crime scene. I decided it was best, at least for right now, to follow in the snow footsteps of the feral cat.

Chapter 12
More Ghost Hunting

"Okay, here's the plan. I'll unlock the house and the admissions bay in the garage. Now, to be honest, there was some kinetic ghost activity going on upstairs in the abandoned apartment. Take Karma. We'll meet up later to look for signs of the tunnel entrance outside."

When I let Bryce know about the odd goings-on in the admissions office—even suggesting paranormal activity—it didn't seem to faze him, so I took that as a good sign.

Peace and I started our tunnel search in the mansion's Craftsman dining room. This room oozed opulence with its floor-to-ceiling mahogany panels. The Oriental carpet was Turkish, one of the original pieces of art belonging to the Pittock family. I marveled at the workmanship as I pored over the paneling, tapping and prodding for a secret compartment. There was some silver displayed in a case with little pickle forks and odd nutcrackers. In a time without the Internet or cable for television, the residents of early Portland would entertain with a splendid dinner. *Sometimes I think I was born in the wrong era.* But then I remembered the sleeping porches upstairs off the bedrooms, used because fresh air was considered beneficial for health, the best that could be done without antibiotics like penicillin.

I hit a dead-air pocket in my tapping and uttered, "Aha."

Running my hand around the edge of what looked like a cabinet, I used my finger to find a latch. On the top I felt a little lever and pushed. *Success*. The cabinet door opened.

Peace was beside me, shining a flashlight into the narrow shelving. "What we have here," she said to me, "is storage for expensive silver to hide it from the help."

Sure enough, that was what this vintage compartment was for. I tapped on the back of the shelving through the delicate spiderwebs that had been undisturbed for a long time. *Tap, tap, tap.* It was solid.

"Well," I said, "that explains the oral history. This is the secret compartment, but it isn't a tunnel or the entrance to a priest's hole." Disappointed, I made another suggestion. "Let's see if there are any ghosts about."

We took the elevator to the third floor since our boots were wet and the stairs would be slippery, with their California marble, chosen for the ritzy look but not for practicality in the wet Pacific Northwest.

Opening the door, we stepped inside my office, also known as Henry's former study. There was nothing of a ghostly presence as far as I could tell. "Empty," Peace said, affirming my sixth-sense take. That's when I looked over at the vintage cubbies that were along one edge of the office wall.

"I think I'm going to tap inside these compartments," I said. "And then let's see how Bryce and Karma have made out in the admissions upstairs apartment." I went from left to right, like reading a book, with my *tap, tap, tap*. When we finally got through all the cubbies, all I'd gained was a kink in my back. I got up off the floor—the last row I'd tried—and shrugged.

"This is all about a process of elimination, looking for an unknown entrance to the house," I said. "At least I've crossed two possibilities off my list. That makes for a stronger case that the murder was committed by one of the people at the gala that night, though, so I need to dig into a motive. But for now, let's check on the others and see if we can find the path Helen told me about."

Outside, the snow was still falling. It was blowing on heavy gusts of wind and accumulating in drifts. For Portland, this was severe winter weather. We made our way to the admissions bay, where Bryce had turned on the overhead heater. Admissions could be a pretty good job, views of the gardens and all, until the temperature fell into the thirties. That's when the heater felt really good. And right now, for that matter.

Peace and I made our way up the stairs and into the apartment with Bryce. Everything was pretty much the way it had been when I'd walked into it after work. But I'd never seen Bryce this enthusiastic and energetic before. He was now in the middle of the apartment. Karma had already crashed on the dusty couch, and Mac was next to her, watching Bryce binge cleaning—his eyes lit with excitement.

"We can live here."

I heard his collective *we*. "You mean a solution to our rental problem?" I looked around, a bit aghast. *I've lived in worse. I've lived in better.* It was going to need some serious cleaning, and then there was the question as to whether it would be approved by the board—and whether it had power—and I wasn't sure if the toilet flushed—and actually, I wasn't even sure if there was a bathroom.

Everyone was looking at me, waiting.

Bryce, his face lit with enthusiasm; Peace, with a knowing smile, like she'd seen the future; Karma, with her eyes filled with contentment (two humans are better than one); and Mac, with his big Scottish grin.

I shrugged. "Okay, I'll see what I can do. Maybe I can pull some strings to make it happen." After all, it would make for a short walk to work each day. "Do you know the park closes the gate at nine in the evening to all car traffic—up or down?"

Nothing I said at this point was going to dissuade Bryce from his apartment find. And granted, I knew he'd been looking harder than I had—Craigslist, Zillow, and word-of-mouth friend inquires.

And maybe besides cleaning it and moving in, I could rationalize it with the need for more security on the property. Maybe I could even convince the powers that be that we could stay for free in exchange for security. The more I thought about it, the more I warmed up to the idea. There were only some issues with ghosts hanging around and maybe a tunnel to the mansion, which we didn't even know if it existed.

That brought me back to reality. "Let's look for the pathway now, and we can come back to the apartment."

With that, one dog, one ghost, and three humans found our way to the entrance to the mansion. "This is how the 1912 Pierce-Arrow would drive to the house to pick up the Pittock family members." I turned and looked at the garden next to the former road. "Down there is where the last family member who lived in the mansion—Peter Gantenbein—described a grotto. If you look over the pathway farther down, you can see concrete supports that were once part of the house and garden."

Inhaling deeply, I took the lead into the garden. With the snow falling and the grounds around the mansion quickly becoming a winter wonderland, it looked like an enchanted forest with a castle. I wasn't worried about our footsteps. The new snow would fill in any traces of our exploration.

It was slippery descending to the grotto that had wasted away since the City built the new road access, but it didn't take long to get to the pillars that marked the little clearing where Helen and Owen had reportedly lit up.

Flakes were coming down as we worked our way farther down the overgrown pathway, revealing a concrete foundation and a securely boarded-over entry or window or something. I wracked my brain to figure out where this part of the structure would connect to the house. It was maybe around the furnace room, or perhaps the former wood storage, where we now housed Christmas decorations. I couldn't figure out how the rooms aligned with any kind of opening in the house.

"I'm going back inside to see if I can understand where this corresponds to the inside of the mansion."

"I'm headed back to that super apartment," Bryce said. "I'll look for a tunnel entrance there, too."

He went back with Karma, while Mac, Peace, and I went into the mansion. We went down the California marble stairs, and then to the left, to the back rooms, into the furnace room. My mind was like a map of the exterior as we combed through the interior. We looked behind shelving and storage, stumped. Nothing appeared like an opening for a tunnel. Next, we went into Henry's vault room and tapped on the concrete. This room was like a bunker with the single bare bulb dangling from the ceiling and no window. The only entrance was through the door.

We found nothing. If the room had secrets, it was keeping them.

And finally, we tried the Christmas storage area that snaked along under the front of the house. I knew that during the day, the decorative colored glass above us let natural light into the space, like I'd seen in the old photographs of Portland where the bubbled glass was embedded in the sidewalks.

We found an entrance for the firewood chute, but otherwise, we came up empty. It was getting late, and we weren't any closer to a solution.

I looked toward Peace. "Anything on a psychic level here?" I asked. I wasn't getting any kind of message.

Peace assumed a tree yoga pose. "No restless spirits in the house. Actually, I'm not detecting any ghosts at all, except for that handsome Highlander."

Mac smiled.

"Where did they all go?" I asked, chagrined. Our ghost-hunting expedition had been a bust.

"Not to worry," Peace said. "It's not over until it's over."

Chapter 13
Holiday Happenings

I NEEDED A FAVOR. I got on the phone, since mostly everything was still closed from the storm. The good news was that it was getting warmer. There was a constant *drip, drip, drip* of melting snow, and people were smiling, walking, and drinking coffee. Some cars were on the road, but since Portland wasn't serious about snowplows, the city was in its usual wait-until-it-melts mindset before everything would get back to normal.

What I didn't have was a lot of time. Winter weather had arrived, and I had a show to arrange for the Pittock Mansion members who looked forward to the mansion being dressed to the hilt once a year for holiday fun. The favor I needed was to get the entertainment arranged as soon as possible for the holiday evening in a few weeks. So, I rang Eric to see if he could assemble a quick ensemble for Dickens's classic *A Christmas Carol*.

It's a fairly short production, and the mansion was a natural setting for it. I planned to have the patrons walking into a new scene in each room—the Ghosts of Christmas Past, Present, and Future. I envisioned them as mini-presentations of the original ghost scenes, continued throughout the day of the holiday preview, with short breaks for the actors, of course. Plus, we already had a houseful of ghosts, so it seemed apropos.

"I'll see what I can do," Eric said.

Once that was in the works, I was able to begin to ponder the apartment above the admissions bay. Bryce and I were ready to start the cleaning. This time, Karma had to stay home. I hadn't seen Mac and believed that he was still courting Nina, and Peace had an alien caucus to attend to. After Bryce and I cleaned, I hoped to still have some time to log in a few hours of work in my office. The day was beginning on a bright note, as we huffed up the hill toward Pittock Mansion and my cell phone rang.

"Got the results back from the lab," Trinity said, her voice somber.

"And...?"

"They got a print off the playbill."

This is what I'd hoped for. I knew crime techs slobbered over the chance to pull a print off paper, and a lot of creepy criminals forget and leave fast-food bags and the like in cars or at the crime scene.

"They got a positive match for Allie Campbell-Stone. She'd been fingerprinted for her real estate licensure, so she was in the system."

So, it was most likely her playbill that I'd found.

How did it get in the tunnel under the pizza restaurant?

"Anything else?" I asked.

"Nothing else. You got your protection with you?" she asked. She was talking about the amulet, not a condom.

"In my pocket."

"Good. Keep it with you all the time."

Bryce and I set to work on the task of cleaning. There is something about sorting, scrubbing, and generally putting things in order that gives me a holy sense of purpose. I'd done this for my brother's office in Sedona, and whenever I have a problem and an answer doesn't present itself right away, at least the physical task of cleaning helps clear my mind. And if that doesn't happen, I can still stand back and admire the results.

Bryce volunteered to clean the bathroom. I knew he was truly committed toward residency in the garage apartment to tackle such a task. I started in the kitchen, cleaning off the surfaces and sorting through old paper *Oregonian*s.

Soon I was sidetracked reading news about events from decades ago, and I was amused at the prices in the advertisements. Meier & Frank, the department store of the time, was a major advertising contributor. That jogged a memory from some of the Pittock family correspondence I'd read. When the first decorator looked at the sixteen thousand square feet of mansion, she recommended some furnishings that were not from that store. The next letter in that series stated something about all future furniture being purchased from Meier & Frank.

I could see Henry Pittock upstairs in his office, negotiating a deal with Meier or Frank about the chance to decorate the lavish mansion. I came back to earth after Bryce emerged from the bathroom with a whiff of bleach in the air. "Coming out for a break," he said and then proceeded to pull newspapers into a recycle bin.

I took to cleaning the kitchen sink and soon found myself sneezing. "I think we've disturbed decades of dust mites," I said and excused myself to go outside for some fresh air.

Later that day, I was ready to call the caterers when I decided to go for a one-on-one interview. My sass was in high gear, and I had things that needed my attention. Thinking about the night of the gala murder, I questioned why Mr. Baker had asked me to change the catering company to Elephants Delicatessen since we usually used another establishment. It was too tempting *not* to investigate, and Elephants wasn't far.

Upon entering the eatery—open and doing a brisk business—I ordered a turkey-and-cheddar sandwich with a cup of tomato-and-basil soup. At a corner table, I ate and observed the staff. My mission was to see if I recognized any of the five employees who'd worked the night of the gala. It wasn't my lucky day, though, because everyone who buzzed around the café was a new face to me. After I finished, I went up to the cashier. "I'd like to talk to someone about catering a holiday event at Pittock Mansion."

The strawberry-blonde cashier—with a charming purple streak in the front of her coiffed hair—showed me to the manager's office.

Now in a tidy but cramped office, I announced my purpose to a man sitting at a desk. "I'm the event planner for the Pittock Mansion, and I need to arrange the food and crew to work at the holiday preview. Our theme this year is old-time Portland. As far as staffing, we need more help on-site than the last event because we'll have more guests. I think you had five at the prior gala?"

He looked at his iPad and tapped it to life. "We had four people, but I can add three more for the upcoming holiday party. Will that work?"

"Yes," I said, "and I'd like the same crew, if possible."

He tapped more on the iPad. "I have your event reserved, and I'll be in touch about the food."

Five people at the gala had represented themselves as catering staff. One of them didn't belong.

At home, I slithered into a little black dress and decided on the silver hoop earrings, red lipstick, and super-high heels. I grabbed the lab cop's business card and hailed a cab since I couldn't walk more than two blocks in heels and parking would be impossible. The last time I'd been at Kells in downtown Portland, well, I'd had to slip away from a particularly difficult man.

I had Trinity's amulet in my cleavage, and the dress was so tight, I believed I *might* be able to have a drink without splitting the seams. Once I'd been transported, I sauntered up to the bar and slung my tiny beaded purse in front of me. I gave the bartender my order—Scotch. It didn't take long for the lab cop from the DRT scene to sit down on the barstool next to me; I was fishing for information, and he was casting for a good time. Sometimes I had to wiggle my principles for what I wanted. Besides, it was only a drink.

Mac appeared suddenly, looking protective.

The lab cop's eyes were already bloodshot, and his words were beginning to slur; he'd apparently had several drinks before I arrived. I guessed that cleaning up after dead bodies could get to a person. I tried to have some compassion, even though I'm not fond of cops. The word *charity* popped into my mind.

"How are things going at work?" I asked. "Anything new?"

It was not particularly clever, but it was where I wanted the conversation to go. I guessed he probably needed a therapist more than a date, and he immediately took the bait.

"There's a new consultant at work, and he's particularly annoying. Sharpshooter, knows languages, and some kind of medicine healer or something. He worked undercover, but now he's been called in as a *special consultant* to help with a Portland case linked with the Warm Springs reservation. Higher-ups talk about him like he can walk on water."

This new information caused my heart to skip a beat. I'd taken a sip of my Scotch and started to cough. Mac tapped me on my back—or at least he tried, but of course, nothing happened.

"So, what's the new guy's name?" I finally asked.

"Dan something. From Sedona."

My heart backflip-fluttered hard in my chest. Sedona. Native American consultant working with the Portland police. Sharpshooter.

"What kind of car does he drive?"

He looked at me, surprised. "A truck, I think, a Ranger. Why?"

It had to be my Danny. I dropped a twenty-dollar bill into the glass for the Scotch and a tip. "Got to go," I said as I whittled myself off the barstool. "Early to work tomorrow."

Mac followed me out to the street where I called for a cab. "Well, Mac," I said, "it appears that a person from my past has come back into my present."

As the cab inched up to the curb to pick me up and take me home, I looked back inside the bar through the large street window. The cop was cozy with a brunette who'd taken my place on my former barstool. "Good, she can take him home."

Chapter 14
The Next Thing

THE MENU FOR THE HOLIDAY event would be fresh salmon with dill; roasted turnips, potatoes, and brussels sprouts; grilled chicken (at an auction or regal event, there's always a chicken option); and a vegetarian option.

But my mind was simmering about the catering crew.

Even as my thoughts spun about the possibility of discovering the imposter, I was thinking about Danny. I knew he'd had experience in law enforcement, but I never expected that he'd leave the Navajo reservation, where he was working with a Navajo medicine man. That's when I'd met him and he saved my life. Actually, he kept me from dying, twice; however, our relationship melted like wax in the hot Arizona desert sun from a strain I preferred not to ruminate about, and I never thought our paths would cross again. And now this.

My emotions about Danny erupted through every fiber of my being.

Most boyfriends were usually pretty easy for me to let go of. I blamed that on the events in my early life—a mother who disappeared at an early age and I didn't know if she was alive or not, and a father who had done his best but had also left me when he died. That's when Aunt Thelma stepped up and took care of me, giving me stability in my life. My brother, Ryan, who was older, took off on his own path. He'd found his passion in the theater, and with the proceeds of his inheritance, he invested in Sedona with the Shakespearean outdoor theater. Things were going well for him and the plays.

The sheriff of Aunt Thelma's small coastal town of Manzanita, Griffin, had been like a dad to me. I thought he should probably be up for sainthood because I'd pushed him away so many times, and he came back with patience while I was like a feral girl. Aunt Thelma was more like my mother's side of the family, which had a legacy of sixth-sense psychic abilities. I clearly inherited the gene for it, but I'd spent most of my life in denial, just trying to be normal to fit in to a small town.

It was after Aunt Thelma's death that I was dispatched to Ireland, courtesy of her last will and testament, to find a long-lost relation, a woman named Nora. I'd found her on the remote Beara Peninsula, and in doing so, I acknowledged my own destiny toward my psychic abilities. For me, this was evolving, and I'd missed the opportunity to learn from Aunt Thelma. All this contributed to where I was now—with a job I loved but a tendency to run away from the past, especially if things got too difficult. And that's not even including the divorce proceedings after I married too young, or that my husband was a clinical narcissist and a hard-core passive-aggressive—and somewhere on the psychopath spectrum when he'd died.

The telephone rang, bringing me out of my life review. It was the manager at Elephants. "I have the holiday event menu ready for sampling," he said. "Tomorrow at noon?"

"Got it," I said and marked it on my calendar.

My next task was to get more of the overstock pulled from the furnace room. The museum store needed bottled water, trail mix, mustard pretzels, magnets, and Pittock Christmas ornaments. As I extracted myself from my chair, the phone rang again.

"Pittock Mansion, Lizzy O'Malley," I answered.

"Can we talk?"

Those three little words stopped me in my tracks. Just when you think you've recovered from the hurts of the past, you realize how vulnerable your heart is.

I wasn't sure how long I'd paused. Finally, I said, "Danny."

I was at a loss, so he filled the void. "Let's meet tonight. I have some things that I need to tell you."

I'd gotten home, let Karma have a walk, and changed into my black leggings, a long and lean sweater in a dark-blue color that made my eyes pop, and cute black leather boots without too much heel. I applied makeup and finished the hot, sexy, all-pulled-together look with my silver hoop earrings. I needed to look even more improved from the last time I'd seen him because I wanted to project that I'd done just fine—excellent—without him. My ego was in play, as if I were headed into a poker game with a high-stakes pot.

I was on my way out the door to meet Danny when I felt something dangerous was lurking, but my intuition wasn't working like it had been, or maybe I was anxious about the meet-up. My amulet was with me in my bag, and I clenched the strap tighter to my side. *Do I skip my meeting with Danny? Or do I push on?* I waited, scanning the scene around me for the source of my apprehension.

After a few minutes, the foreboding feeling vanished. In the past, if I was in danger, the hairs would rise on my arms, and sometimes I'd even get a heavy metallic taste in my mouth—then I knew it was really bad.

I shrugged it off and made my way to the Rams Head pub on Northwest Hoyt Street. It's one of several eateries started by the McMenamin brothers, Portland siblings who buy old buildings around Oregon and southwest Washington, finishing them with an eclectic, whimsical taste in free-spirited decorations. The repurposed buildings could have been funeral parlors, schools, poorhouses—nothing was unreasonable to be redeveloped by the McMenamins.

I was seated in a booth by the window and wanted to catch a glimpse of Danny before he saw me. The dreaded past review spun in my mind, especially him and that Chavez woman, a beautiful, elegant, and exotic competitor. Danny and I had kissed under the stars on the reservation, and in the warmth of the remaining heat from the day, Danny and I had made love. But there was a problem that I hadn't known at the time. And from my point of view, it was that I gave my heart to Danny when he wasn't free to receive it. That, and he was mixed up in some kind of reservation scandal with jewelry that should have been original and made on the reservation and instead was fake and made a person's wrist turn green.

Of course, before I'd been able to sort it out, and in a bit of a temperamental mood, I'd metaphorically and literally exploded some dynamite, ruining a fair amount of the space where the jewelry was stashed, and then later Danny saved my life, with a sharpshooter's eye and steady hand. Needless to say, I was conflicted about Danny. But he'd said today that he needed to talk to me, and he was direct and urgent. I recalled the old medicine man who'd brought Danny back to his spiritual roots and claimed that things were not as they appeared. His words whispered in the echoes of my memory, and I somehow knew that there would be an answer one day. And maybe it was today.

When Danny came through the door, I inhaled. He was even more attractive—rugged and handsome—and then a part of me went soft inside. But I kept the skeptical hardness on the outside, using the trade of an actor to hide my feelings.

As he slipped into the booth, I could feel all the eyes in the pub on him. *I mean, he's one hot guy.*

"Hey," I said, lamely.

Really, is that the best you can do?

He looked into my eyes like he could see my soul. Actually, since he was a spiritual healer, I think he could. Then he smiled. And Danny had a smile that could light up the world. At least, it could light up mine.

We started with the trivial, and since that felt pretty good, we launched into the harder stuff, the details that can drive a wedge between people making an effort to reconnect in a relationship. "I couldn't tell you before," Danny began, "that I was working undercover on the reservation. The jewelry was just the tip of it; we had more drug rings on the reservation, and I couldn't tell you that."

My thoughts roiled. I squirmed around on my faux-leather bench seat. "So, what about Chavez?"

My green-eyed jealously kicked into high gear. I could forgive him if he had to keep the secret from me about his work, but I didn't think I could forgive him about that woman. After all, my former husband had cheated on me, and it was a raw nerve of betrayal.

"Fair question." He took my hand. "The truth is that I was involved with her until I met you. Then, it was over between us. She sensed that something was wrong, and I couldn't jeopardize the other members of the undercover team, and I couldn't tell you then. But I'm telling you now."

I looked at his muscular hand in mine. I was ready to yield and melt into the moment, but then my own guilt washed over me, and I took my hand back and put it in my lap.

Danny looked at me, trying to sense the reason for my withdrawal. "Do you still have feelings for me? Is there someone else who's come into your life?"

I squirmed under his gaze. *Well, two guys that I can remember.* There was John Hall, the cop in Sedona, who'd wined and dined me, and in a moment of complete confusion, I'd succumbed to the passion. And then there was dear sweet Jimmy in Belfast, a kind, loving, and *temporary* soul mate.

The thing about Danny was that he seemed to already know and forgive. Not psychic, like my family, but a healer who had once returned the fragments of my soul to me when I'd needed the kind of medicine not sold in a store or pharmacy.

"I knew our paths would cross again," he said.

"I'm glad they have."

I returned my hand to his, and I knew he still had something else to tell me. "The murder at the Pittock," he began. "I need you to know that Allie Campbell-Stone was sedated, smothered, and then staged in that miniature elevator."

"Stuffed," I corrected. "She was a petite little thing to have fit at all."

He regarded me with interest. "The curator's death was the same MO. Maybe done by the same person. The toxicology report indicates they were given a high dose of a sleeping drug beforehand." He gave me his cell phone number and then looked me in the eye.

I saw love and concern, but he knew better than to smother my independence. We'd worked through that issue in Sedona. "If you suspect anything, let me know, *personally*."

Chapter 15
Break-In

SOME OF THE TOP SELLERS at the Pittock Mansion museum store were coloring books for adults. A creative way to relieve stress, the Tiffany-themed books were a particular favorite, designed out of translucent paper, ready to color inside the lines to make it look like the famous stained glass. I checked the inventory on the computer, and the number that came up wasn't what I thought we had down in the overstock in the furnace room, so my next task was to physically check it.

I dodged the boxes that needed crushing for recycling, and the bubble wrap, left after I'd unpacked an order, and the small mote carved out of the concrete floor that made the 1914 furnace look like a castle. Small amounts of water collected in it.

Unlocking a bin, I found the coloring books—and there appeared more than the computer indicated. I used the walkie-talkie to confirm that I was bringing more out to the store. "Do we need anything else?" I asked Molly.

"Nope," she said through the broken static of the low-tech device.

Puzzled over the difference in inventory versus the computer, I jumped when Mac suddenly appeared. Mac pointed up like he was attempting to communicate with me about something topside. I wished he could talk. We'd have a nice heart-to-heart about so many things. But I guessed in the state of things, I was lucky to have Mac. I hadn't felt that way when he'd first appeared and followed me to my bed-and-breakfast and on the train, but now we had settled into a nice little routine. And he did seem like an ounce of protection, although I really felt like I could take care of myself.

"What is it you are trying to tell me?" I asked, even though I knew I wasn't going to get a response. He gestured for me to follow him. Since my task of gathering up the overstock to take to the store was done, I capitulated. "I'll follow you, Mac, as soon as I take these to Molly."

It occurred to me that my psychic warnings hadn't been as active since I'd met Mac. *Could the microchip be limiting my abilities?* That thought was fairly unpleasant.

I dropped off the coloring books at the store and noticed Molly's outfit was mousy—a gray dress that looked too large for her. It didn't look like she was wearing makeup either. *Maybe she's coming down with a cold?*

"It seems like there's a discrepancy in our inventory—the computer versus what we have on hand. Did Mr. Baker mention anything to you about a glitch or that he'd noticed anything?" I asked.

Molly shook her head and brought a piece of Kleenex to her nose. "He kept that to himself. I'm glad we have more of the coloring books, though. I'd sold out." She turned around and went back to her dusting and restocking.

Mac had disappeared but reappeared on the pathway that led to the stairs and to the gate lodge; it was closed for the day since a volunteer had canceled. When I got to the front door, I found the source of Mac's urgency. The old door—both wood and glass, like many original home doors—was broken at the window. Checking inside, the quaich was still nestled against its dark velvet bag, but the dueling pistols and the case with all the accessories were gone.

Damn. Someone had boosted half of our new exhibit.

I whipped out my cell phone and called the police. Then I made a private call to Danny like I'd promised, and I alerted Molly about the theft via the squawking walkie-talkie. My next call was to the City to arrange a replacement of the door window. After that, I locked the door for a small ounce of protection. And finally, I called the museum's insurance company.

The volunteers commenced with the traditional decking of the holiday rooms at the Pittock. The mansion was closing to the public for two days while a whirlwind of decorating activity transpired, and I was looking forward to the different kind of chaos that it would bring. The theme this year was old Portland—motifs of Stumptown.

The library was getting a makeover in all-natural decorations. *My favorite room.* The Christmas tree was to one side, allowing the natural view to shine. It included the tip of Mount Hood—if you were willing to peek around some hundred-year-old Douglas fir growth outside. The decorations were all natural—no glitz—in a nod to the forty-plus acres of forested property surrounding the house.

"Looks great," I said before I dashed off to the next room like a hummingbird.

I didn't have to go far. At the formal entrance of the mansion stood an easel with a picture of one of the former mayors of Portland, the iconic Bud Clark. He was a barkeep before he was mayor, and in this photograph, Clark was holding a can of Budweiser beer. The caption: *This Bud's for You.* This was before the elite microbrew culture had exploded into Portland's scene. A volunteer was setting out an old tweed hat that had belonged to the former mayor along with other Bud Clark memorabilia. Missing, however, was another iconic photograph of the former mayor in a raincoat, flashing a statue, with the caption *Expose Yourself to Art*. I could not help but think, *Politically correct*.

I swept down the hallway on light feet to the Turkish smoking room. The construction of this circular chamber, including the wood floor, was a testament to the craftsmen who built the house. The ceiling was plaster and painted in the most detailed pattern, in hues of blue with bits of red and gold. A volunteer was smoothing out the folds of a dress on a mannequin. The frock sparkled with rhinestone bling like a disco ball. Actually, when I looked up, I realized one of those hung from a drapery rod. The room was a quintessential glitter fest with a nod to Portland's most famous drag queen, Darcelle XV.

"Nice," I said to the volunteer, remembering the time when I'd watched Darcelle's show on 3rd Avenue.

My next stop was the dining room. It revealed a classic holiday image of Portland with roses on a Christmas tree and miniature paintings with the same motif. Portland is the Rose City, and Georgiana Pittock was the founder of the Rose Festival, still celebrated in June with parades and a fair. From there, I passed through the butler's pantry. The kitchen and the refrigerator room—an entire room devoted to an early version of a refrigerator instead of the typical early icebox—flowed with a dragon boat theme.

Taking a deep breath, I was gliding on air. The transformation of the mansion for the holidays made me happy. I took a quick time-out from the decorations and called Peace on my cell phone.

"I need an extra pair of eyes and some sixth-sense acumen at the holiday preview party on Sunday. I don't want a repeat of the events at the gala. Will you help?"

"No problem. I'll be there," she said.

We cut the conversation short because Peace was on her way to a new age bookstore on Northwest 23rd Avenue.

I took the stairs to preview the second-floor decorations. One of the sleeping porches was filled with Meier & Frank memorabilia. The decorations included a collage of the department store monorail that children rode around in the fantasy of Toyland. I was sad to think that the downtown Portland department store had since been sold and the upper floors converted to a trendy bar with a view, but this display brought it back in some small way.

From the sleeping porch, I entered Henry's bedroom and peeked at Henry Pittock's bathroom. Mr. and Mrs. Pittock had their own sleeping rooms, as was the custom at the time. Henry's bathroom had one of the best views in the house, facing Mount Hood. He also had a rather unheard-of feature for the time, a foot soaker. Here he could sit and splash his feet in hot water, viewing the mountain that he summited several times. In this room, one of the favorite guest places in the mansion, was a shower with multiple controls and heads—a regal spa for the era. The volunteer decorators were busy in here, using sheets of Plexiglas and small figures to convert the foot wash into a miniature skating rink, like the one in the famous Lloyd Center, a shopping mall in Northeast Portland.

All in all, things were going smashingly, with all the other upstairs rooms good to go.

That being the case, I dashed downstairs to grab some cleaning supplies for Bryce. The situation as roommates would change now that Danny was back in the picture. I hoped to spend a lot more time with Danny. Plus, Bryce confided that he'd met someone at a cannabis dispensary; he'd fallen hard and fast.

"The ginger-haired woman at the shop told me that I might see things differently if I ate these infused candy edibles," Bryce had told me one night. "But most importantly, I think I've fallen in love with her and want her to have my babies."

"How long have you known her?"

"About fifteen minutes. But I expect to see her again tomorrow."

I smiled to myself. Nina and Mac, coupled. Bryce and the ginger-haired woman. Danny and me. *Things are looking up for the holidays.*

After taking the cleaning supplies to the apartment over the garage, I stopped at the museum store, now displaying Christmas ornaments for purchase. Sales were historically excellent over the holiday preview.

We had vintage-style toys for sale this year. There were Brio train pieces and wooden yo-yos as well as dolls and tea party sets—for indoors or outdoors. Puzzles were also big, as were board games and Pittock Mansion coffee mugs. I hummed a Christmas carol under my breath.

For this event, the caterers were to set up food in the game rooms, to either side of the basement room. Along with Christmas spirits of Dickens, the wine and beer spirits were to be stationed in the entry hall, in front of the elevator doors. As a nod to the gate lodge history, desserts were to be Scottish shortbread and scones along with fresh fruit.

I planned to take up the Scottish motif with a lovely plaid skirt that mimicked the Skene family's traditional plaid in the gate lodge. I'd found the darling short skirt in tartan at a little boutique—kismet. I would add some black leggings and a classic black sweater, along with Aunt Thelma's pearl strand necklace and some bright-red lipstick. It was all coming together.

Chapter 16

A Detour toward Trouble

I HAD THE NEXT DAY off, and I was surprised by a tapping on my door. Peace was at the threshold with two hot coffees and a pink box of Voodoo Doughnuts.

"I've been thinking," Peace began. "We should talk to the developer's wife."

I shrugged. I wasn't sure why, but I knew that Peace had her sixth-sense activated, and I'd always been a bit of a voyeur when it came to visiting rich people's homes. I'd thought about studying architecture before I'd turned toward drama in college, and I still loved to drive through parts of Southwest Portland to look at the stoic homes that screamed of Portland money. I didn't want one myself—I didn't make enough to put a dent in the property taxes of owning one of these classic homes—but I sure enjoyed the opportunity to sniff around them.

I looked up the address of the Crookshanks from our membership records, but I was already pretty sure I knew where they lived. It was one of those landmark homes on Portland's west side.

We took a leisurely drive to the developer's house. Even from the outside, we could see through to the other side of the house with floor-to-ceiling windows that could have been a centerpiece article for *Architectural Digest* magazine.

Motion caught my eye as I waited at the door, where I had politely knocked. Peace stood behind me. I halfway expected hired help to come to the door, although Portland wasn't awash with that kind of servitude. Mrs. Crookshank opened the door in a plum-colored velour jogging suit. Her eyes peered over the top of her reading glasses, and then she glanced at the *No Solicitors* sign on the bottom right of the window next to her door before recognition registered on her face although portions of it appeared to be frozen from a recent Botox treatment.

"What do you want?" she asked with an air that reminded me that she was from money.

"To extend a personal invitation to the Pittock holiday preview," I said. "You and your husband are such important gold-star members." I handed over the seasonal tickets for the holiday preview that would normally have been delivered via email. "The mansion wants one-on-one outreach to our outstanding member contributors." In reality, the development department was a tiny cubicle in a dust-filled corner closet on the third floor—the board was always thinking about hiring a person.

To that, she opened the door a crack wider. "I remember you at the gala," she said.

"Yes, and my new assistant and I would like to ask you a few questions about the catered gala event that you last attended. I wasn't able to hand out questionnaires at the end of the evening. The mansion needs trustworthy feedback from someone who can *accurately* rate the food and beverage service. We are always working to improve and appreciate your assistance."

Okay, I was in little-white-lie mode.

She stepped away from the door and invited us inside, where the view was even more stunning. Next to the door was a huge telescope, the type you might expect at a multimillion-dollar ocean property. She motioned for us to sit on the sofa between Pottery Barn aqua-colored pillows while she mixed herself a drink at an elaborate wet bar to the right. I heard the ice clink in the glass and watched what followed—a generous shot of gin and some tonic.

After she had her cocktail, she reclined in a cream-colored leather chair, and I plunged ahead with on-the-spot malarkey. "Caterers are evaluated after each event, and while we have had some solid feedback about the catered food, we have had mixed reviews about the catering staff."

I'm leading her, but how else do I extract information?

She took a deep drink from her gin and tonic. "The food was fine. I don't remember anything critical about the catering staff. I had a drink in my hand the entire time, and the caterers didn't stand out one way or another—the way you want staff. But the murder of the real estate woman…" Her voice trailed off.

The developer's wife's neck was long and wrinkled. I subconsciously resisted the urge to rub mine.

"Well, my husband knew her," she continued. "That real estate woman was a whore—but he's already moved on to another one, and I've got the best attorney from Gevurtz Menashe working on my divorce," she said, satisfied that she'd conveyed her feelings on the matter.

A brief bit of empathy washed over me. Now the gin and tonic early in the day seemed to be a predictable balm to smooth over her emotions. Divorce is rough. It's tough. And it can make people do unpredictable things. My now-dead husband is a case in point.

I saw in front of me a maligned woman transported to the balcony of life, watching affairs that were hastening change and probably financial distress.

"I'll plan to see you at the holiday preview," I said, thanking her as we got up to leave.

"I doubt it," she answered as she showed us to the door.

After we were at my car, I turned to Peace. "Well? Tell me what you were able to psychically read from her."

"Did you see her aura?"

I'd been able *to see* auras, but ever since I'd channeled Mac, my psychic energies were impaired. I couldn't explain it, or I would have mentioned it to Peace before now. "My sixth sense is faulty," I confessed. "I think the microchip and channeling Mac are interfering with my psychic psychometry, and I couldn't see her aura. I need the chip removed."

"You might not see that handsome Highlander ghost again."

I'd grown fond of Mac, like I would a protective brother, but now I played devil's advocate. "The problem is, I'm in the dark, and I need to fix it. This psychic stuff doesn't come with an instruction manual." I started the ignition and looked over at the neighbors' homes, several millions of dollars, each of them—these were the kind of people who helped the money flow into the Pittock Mansion.

"What about her aura?" I asked.

"It's a dusky color, dirty," Peace said.

"Which means she can't be trusted?"

"Maybe."

There was a ringtone from my phone; it was Danny. I wondered if my Navajo medicine man boyfriend could see me in real time with his visions.

"Peace is with me," I said as I picked up the call.

He paused for a second. "Well, Jonathan Applegate is dead. I don't have anything more right now, but both of you, be careful." With that, Danny clicked off.

I looked out at the view toward the east side, trying to center myself. "You heard?" I asked Peace.

She nodded. "Three people from the night of the event are dead."

I had my hands on the steering wheel, in the safe ten-and-two-o'clock placement. But I didn't feel safe. In fact, I decided to take charge with my next plan.

"My psychic-ness is failing me, and I need to fix it."

"How?" Peace asked.

"At a tattoo parlor. Want to come along?"

Chapter 17
The Chip

IT'S ALWAYS DIFFICULT FINDING a parking space off Burnside in the Old Town neighborhood of Portland. After circling several blocks, I said my parking space prayer—*Holy Mary full of grace, help me find a parking place.*

I didn't like to call on Mary's grace unless I really needed her, but I felt like right now, I did. And my prayer was answered as a four-wheel-drive oversized vehicle pulled out of a space. I parked and set the brake while I sent my thank-you to the universe.

I put my Visa card into the closest parking meter, printed out a tag, and put it in the sidewalk side of the car's window to avoid a scolding or worse from parking enforcement.

A little bell jingled as I opened the front door. Out from behind the curtain came a tallish man with long hair and a thin face.

"Can I help you?"

"I don't have an appointment," I said. I'd expected my friend to be here, not a stranger. "Where's Ronnie Parker?"

"Mexico."

I couldn't let a stranger remove a microchip that shouldn't be there. As I almost turned to leave, Peace stared intently at the ink art.

"I'll get this one," she said, tapping her finger on the image of a bagpiper. It seemed that it should take more than a minute for a decision to have a tattoo.

"Where do you want it?" he asked.

"Right here." She pointed to her right boob, as she lifted her shirt, and she wasn't wearing a bra.

When Peace was finished with her new tatt, she smiled like a cat who had swallowed a canary.

I focused on my next plan. "I'm going to the Lakewood Center to ask some more questions."

I broke off from my monologue when I noticed the tattoo artist with his hand on Peace's shoulder.

"This is Gary," Peace said to me. "We're thinking about dinner. Want to join us?"

Peace and Gary. Mac and Nina. Bryce and the redhead in the cannabis shop. Danny and me. If this were a Shakespearean comedy, the bard would smile at all the coupling.

"I'll take a pass." *Three's a crowd.*

I was on my phone as soon as I got inside my car. "Do you want to come over to my place for dinner tonight?" I asked Danny as soon as he picked up my call; we were both so busy that we hadn't had much time to put the frosting on the cake of our renewed relationship.

"What time?" he asked.

"Seven."

"See you then."

I pulled out a minute before my time was up and waved to the parking enforcement person.

Eric Thomson hugged me as soon I came in through the theater doors. I didn't hesitate with the news. "Two more people are dead—Anthony Baker and the board chair, Jonathan Applegate."

Eric's face mirrored my own, dark. "The cast is all together."

I knew most of the actors from the variety of theater gigs I'd done with them in the past. Part of what was driving me was that I kept thinking that something had slipped past me the night of the murder and someone here might have the answer. Plus, the tea-reading results kept nagging at me that there was something I'd overlooked.

"There are now three people who attended the performance the night of the gala who are dead—murdered. Allie Campbell-Stone, Anthony Baker, and Jonathan Applegate," I began. "And I need some help."

There was nervous twittering.

"If there's anything you remember that you believe might be odd, please contact me."

I saw shrugs. Disappointed, I said my goodbyes to Eric and was at the theater door when Helen came running with her cell phone. Out of breath, she handed me her mobile. "I scrolled through my photos from the night of the gala," she said. "I'd forgotten about this one."

There, behind the spread of the lavish appetizers from the night of the glitter gala, was a shadow of someone hidden in one of the game rooms that were attached to the basement social room like wheel spokes.

"Send it to me, okay?"

As soon as I heard the *ping* of an email, I forwarded the photo to Danny with the text: *The night of the gala. New suspect?*

That night, I took Karma for a quick walk. Then we made our way to the apartment, where she gobbled kibble and lapped up a large amount of water. I used my socks to sop up the remains of her hydration and then threw them into my wash basket, went back into the kitchen barefooted, and opened the refrigerator door with hope that springs eternal—but I knew I didn't have food. Searching through the cupboards, I again came up empty, so I grabbed my coat, slipped on my clogs, and went around the corner to a Thai restaurant. As I carried the brown paper take-out bags inside, Karma looked excited.

"Not for you, girlfriend," I said and patted her on top of the head.

I did a fresh pass over my lips with lip gloss before the doorbell rang.

Danny and I were busy with our lives, but matters of the heart require you to be vulnerable in order to move a relationship forward. "I've got a few more things to tell you," I said as soon as Danny and I were settled on the couch with Karma nuzzled against my leg. "It has to do with a microchip and a detail about the trip to Scotland."

We'd settled in with two fingers of Scotch each, and I told him the quick version about Culloden and the Highland ghost. Being a Navajo spiritual guide, Danny wasn't surprised about a spirit—he'd dream-traveled with me in Arizona, and he had his own stories of where time and space become thin and spirits of ancestors appeared to him.

"Is he here now?" Danny asked. He still wore his heavy winter sweater, and I guessed he was feeling the icy presence of Mac.

"Yes. It's why it's so cold in here. And Mac's pouting because you're here, but he has a girlfriend ghost from Old Town Pizza. Nina's her name, and I think he should go find her right now." I turned to the empty chair—well, it looked empty, but not to me.

I pointed to the front door for emphasis and added the universal shooing motions with my hands when he seemed a little too comfortable. If nothing else, his visiting Nina would improve my heating bill. "And ask your girlfriend what she knows about the Pittock murders."

Mac disappeared, and the room immediately began to warm. "I think I need the chip removed, but I don't know if that will make me lose Mac."

"You said that the Highland ghost protects you? Keeps an eye on you?" Danny said.

"Yep."

"I vote to keep him around."

With that, Danny took me in his arms and pulled me closer—so close that I could hear his heart beat as we made our way to the bedroom. My body knew what came next. And with that, the cold of the winter disappeared, replaced with the heat between us.

Chapter 18
Yoga and the Fire

HAUNTED. I'D HEARD IT FIRST from Molly Murphy on my first day of work at the mansion. "Pictures move around by themselves from room to room; windows open by themselves—especially Henry's bathroom window. Have a talk with him so you don't get blamed. Oh, and then there are the lights that people see come on in the building at night—even though we don't use timers."

That was the thought that kept entering my mind as I started an early morning yoga session before work. I'd been away from my practice for too long. But my reuniting with Danny in a kismet kind of way, and the interference of the chip with my usual premonitions, made me hungry for the benefits of yoga.

I rolled out my mat and went into a child's pose. Oh, the hips were tight, even though I'd had a great hip opener with Danny last night.

With the ethereal sound of the meditation music in the background, I pushed my thoughts to the present. That's the beauty of yoga. It helps clear the mind as well as the body. I rolled onto my back and took my left leg to my chest. I held it and breathed. Then I took my right leg to my chest and held it. I breathed. *Inhale, exhale. Life.*

Life was taken away from Allie Campbell-Stone, Anthony Baker, and Jonathan Applegate.

There I go again. Slipping into the past.

I willed myself to be in the present and rolled into happy baby pose; I forced myself to be present. Warrior, down dog, cat-cow, bridge, and finally, at the end, I released my stress in a puddle of tears.

After a shower and changing into a super-cute new outfit—a black wool skirt, a dark-green sweater with a scarf in a cream background and a paisley pattern that picked up hints of the black and green, along with some vintage rhinestone earrings that I'd found in Southeast Portland at a little boutique on Clinton Street—I rocked at the part of curator and event planner.

Inside the mansion for the workday, I took a quick preview walk around the house to make sure everything was shipshape. Entering Henry's bathroom, I found a window open. It was always the same one. The casements on the windows were vintage and temperamental; it took just the right amount of push, pull, and latch to get them locked. "Is there something you want me to know, Mr. Pittock?"

I waited for an answer but heard nothing, so I took the servant stairs to the basement. In grander times of the past, the staff would move seamlessly through the mansion, from basement to third floor—behind the scenes. *Very* Downton Abbey–*esque.* Now on the bottom floor, I swept through the social room and the back hallway. Just then the lights in the hallway, outside the bathroom doors, hummed, then faded and went bright, like a ghost had a hand on a dimmer switch.

I'd become accustomed to stones speaking to me, the whispers of my dead clan in a Belfast cemetery, and the sensations from objects about their prior owners, but this—this was different.

Tea, tea, tea.

I thought back to the tea reading that seemed ages ago. What was it that I saw in those patterns?

A change in my career—well, that had happened. That I'd be blocked—well, I was about as obstructed as if I were trying to walk through a brick wall. That was exactly the emotion I felt.

The night of the murder—there was something that I'd missed. And in the tea leaves was that mountain and the insurmountable odds that I faced—was currently facing.

My work life felt precise, but other events had me dead-ended. Meeting a ghost on the moor of Culloden, retrieving the artifacts from the Inverness museum, having one half of said artifacts stolen from the gate lodge display, meeting Peace again, rekindling my relationship with Danny, and dealing with three murders that appeared to be linked to the night of the gala.

Still blocked. I couldn't see the sense of it.

I would have liked to have known Henry Pittock in his lifetime. I'd watched an Oregon Public Broadcasting special with Stephen Hawking, and he believed in the theory that there could be the same people we know now but in an alternate reality. If a person stepped right instead of left, one event changed everything; therefore, if various realities were possible, could Peace—with her psychic abilities—communicate outside our universe? And if that's the case, could it be that in another dimension, Henry Pittock hadn't died of the Spanish flu? And if all that was possible, could there be something about me that channeled time in a different way?

117

Somehow, though, it didn't really matter. What mattered was that Allie Campbell-Stone—murdered and stuffed in the dumbwaiter at the mansion—was dead, along with the others. None had appeared to me as ghosts. *Is it because they don't know how to materialize yet? Does it take hundreds of years, like Mac at Culloden, to know how to appear?*

Peace said I had to allow a ghost to manifest. I hoped she was correct, since I dreaded the possibility of conjuring my dead former husband. We'd had insurmountable issues before he'd died, and I wasn't in the mood to carry on any further dialogue with him.

I repeated my question in the empty basement: "Is there something you want me to know, Henry?" But nothing came to me, and nothing flew through the air, no ghost of Henry appeared—just the normal silence of the house before it opened for the day.

After work, I had an errand that shifted to the top of my priorities. My car. Like, maintenance. My ragged windshield wipers could barely take the rain off the windshield without leaving a tapestry of smudges. As I tried to peer through the glowing-ringed hazes of brake lights and traffic signals, I remembered that dreaded night when I was lost in the desert and the Jeep I was riding in went over the edge of a cliff. I'd lived, but that seemed like a lifetime ago with everything else that had happened to me since that night in Arizona.

I think when you don't take the time to process things like grief and change, if you only just plow ahead in life, like I seemed to do, then eventually the emotional work that you've avoided won't wait any longer.

Now, for the second time today, I felt the sobs—a flow of repressed grief—bubbling to the surface, even as I wanted to avoid it. I took a quick turn and found an auto dealership still open. With red-rimmed eyes, I inquired about new windshield wiper blades. The man behind the counter didn't question me about crying regarding an auto part; he just placed a box of Kleenex on the counter and consulted the computer to see if he carried it.

When he appeared with the new wipers, we walked to the parking lot together. The street lamp was rimmed in the glow of Portland rain, almost a beach-like mist. I watched him take the old wipers off the car, revealing the rust on the prongs underneath, hidden, like my own emotions. He wiped them off with some additional Kleenex and—with a slide and a *pop*—replaced the wipers. Good as new. I wished that life was like that: a quick rub, a slide, and a pop, and all was as before.

I heard fire engines in the background, the foreshadowing of trouble. The first engine went by, and then the second, followed by the third.

"Must be a big one," the mechanic said as I finished paying.

I looked over my shoulder at what he saw—plumes of angry gray and black smoke rising from what must have been a big fire. Unfortunately, it was in the direction of my apartment. Slipping into my car, I tried to ready myself to fight through the traffic that had backed up on Burnside. Instead, I got out of my car and went back into the shop.

"Mind if I keep it parked in your lot?" I asked. "I'll come back for it tomorrow."

"No worries," he said.

Walking toward my apartment, a feeling of dread filled me as my heart skipped. The streets were filled with fire trucks, hoses squirting water at my home as flames licked out from the top of the roof.

I was ready to collapse into a whimpering ball of grief at the sight. My dog was inside, and I feared it was too late to save her.

Woof, woof.

I looked through the thick smoke to the line of bystanders and made out the silhouette of Karma with Bryce standing next to her. Next to them was Mac, hand on his blade. I ran over to them, sobs welling, and I hugged Karma, her pink tongue out, panting from the heat of the building's fire.

"What happened?" I asked.

"Someone wants us out, permanently," Bryce said.

There it is.

Bryce went to stay with a friend, but I didn't know where I'd be for the night. I was thinking a hotel, but before I could figure it out, Danny pulled up in his truck. There was a tightness around his eyes. It was as if a black cloak of fabric had been thrown over the whole of Portland, and no light was coming through.

"Stay with me," he said.

Karma didn't wait for my answer. She hopped into the truck, ready for the next adventure and a warm spot to sleep for the night. I got into the Ranger and buried my head in my hands. When I looked up, I saw that Mac had manifested in the bed of the truck. I thought for a second that he couldn't ride in an open bed, but then I remembered that he was already dead, so it wasn't technically breaking any law.

"I'm getting tired of this," I said. Danny took me in his arms as I started to shake. "I almost lost Karma." Big emotional sobs bubbled from my heart. While I was in a state of despair, I reminded myself that I had to use my now-limited psychic abilities to figure out the crimes in order to stop anyone else from getting hurt.

"I know that look on your face," Danny began. He realized that he couldn't stop me from working on this murder puzzle (and who had set fire to my apartment) any more than he could capture the wind in the palm of his hand. He nodded, more to himself than to anyone else. "I'll be there with you, at the holiday party, so when you poke the bees' nest, you'll have some backup."

Danny really was beginning to understand me. *Maybe this relationship is going to work this time.*

What I needed was a supercharged dopamine-producing marathon shopping trip. After all, I didn't have anything to wear except the clothes on my back. "I need retail therapy before we go to your place." Danny turned, and we headed to Northwest 23rd Avenue. In under two hours, I had a sexy little black nightgown—Danny wondered why I even bothered—and mix-and-match clothes that I could squeeze seven days of outfits out of. It wasn't a lot, but it would get me through the workweek. I'd found a lovely cropped wool jacket in a gray color, to lock down a neutral palette with my new wardrobe. I'd found a silky top in mauve and snapped that up along with a pencil skirt in black wool. I even found a duplicate of my plaid skirt that I'd planned to wear for the holiday gala. I didn't find the same black sweater, but I found a lovely black cropped cashmere number that looked even better with the tartan skirt. I bought three pairs of black leggings and one pair in gray. I also found some black and gray pants, and I purchased one of each. At the little boot-and-shoe shop, I found a pair of low black boots that would work with everything along with a gray pair that were more traditional, but they popped with style. Undies and makeup were the last purchases.

"Now, I feel better," I said, catching my breath through the dopamine-charged purchases. I'd used my emergency Visa card. A migraine was to follow when I got the bill, but I had to have clothes to wear, right?

Danny caught my hand and pulled me closer to him in a hug.

There was something about him that made me feel better. Maybe it was because he saved me when he found me in the Arizona desert, but I thought it was a warmth that generated from his soul.

When we got back to the truck, we turned onto Burnside Street and sailed over the bridge and into Southeast Portland in no time. Then we headed south, toward Sellwood, another neighborhood that was growing in leaps and bounds. At one time, it had been its own little city, with the businesses on 13th Avenue as the core of the tiny town. Sellwood was gobbled up by Portland long ago, and now it was one of the popular urban destinations for newcomers.

We stopped at an Italian restaurant, Gino's, where we sipped glasses of Chianti and filled our bellies with pasta. Karma waited patiently in the truck until we came out of the restaurant, and she sniffed wildly at the leftovers. That's when we made one more stop for some organic salmon-and-sweet-potato dog food at New Seasons before we made it back to Danny's townhouse.

"I'm renting while I figure things out," he said to me. This time we were settled between the sheets, me in my cute little black night-gown, Danny in, well, nothing at all. "But it's about to be taken over by a new management company."

I didn't plan to have the nightgown on for long, but it was nice to have a chance for some pillow talk. I really hadn't thought about a long-term relationship with Danny. But then I zoned in on what Danny had said, and it wasn't about the relationship.

"What's the name of the company?"

"Crookshank, I think."

My spaghetti strap was in his hand and coming off my shoulder. I snuggled closer to him. "He's the developer that was at the gala. His wife is divorcing him, but you probably know that."

Danny nodded.

"And now he's gobbling up properties all over the city. My apartment building—now burned—and your townhouse rental."

The other spaghetti strap was off my left shoulder. All conversation would be over as soon as my nightgown was removed.

"So, what happened to Mr. Applegate? You told me he died. I mean, there's gossip at work about it, so I was wondering. A board member also called to let me know he'd passed."

Danny's eyes smiled. He was not thinking about work, and I was having a hard time focusing because I knew that soon the only thing between the two of us was going to be some heavy breathing.

"Mr. Applegate died with a large quantity of sedative, like a sleeping pill, in his system, and he was smothered."

"Murder."

"That's the current theory."

At that, my little black nightie was discarded, and for the rest of the evening, we didn't need to talk.

When the first rays of low winter light came through Danny's townhouse window, I smelled coffee and remembered back to the first time I'd seen him making fresh brew, not long after he'd discovered me sunburned, blistered, and thirsty in the desert. I smiled at the memory as I got into the shower. As the warm water pulsated on me, I lathered up my hair with shampoo and then applied conditioner, and by the time I'd wrapped a towel around me, I was almost ready for my day.

I put on the black pencil skirt and the black leggings, plus the mauve top, and took the tags off with a satisfying *pop-pop*. After I dried my hair and pulled it into a bun on the top of my head, I added the cropped gray jacket and slipped into my new boots.

Not bad, considering it was a post-fire outfit and on sale.

Danny had left a note that he'd see me tonight. I grabbed a piece of toast and some fruit, then called a cab.

When I arrived at my office, Molly was waiting for me with a cup of coffee and a merchandise catalog.

"How are we doing with the store?" I asked.

"I'm about ready with the setup. I have one more tree to do with the newest ornaments delivered yesterday." We decided to add a garden-themed holiday tree to the store merchandise since the forest-motif library was such a hit with the volunteers. "New outfit?" she asked.

I looked down at my ensemble. "I got some things."

"Your scarf will look great with that," she said. That's when I realized that I'd left my Scottish cashmere neck wrap at work last night. I grabbed it and designed it around my neck. *Perfect.*

Molly went to the store, and I checked my email. One was from the board of directors, about the upcoming holiday event and that the entire board would be there. There was also a business line about the need to hire more staff for visitor services. Molly and I were now the only full-time employees, and we were working our volunteers to the bone. Granted, the mansion would be closed in January for maintenance, but we needed help.

The volunteers were finishing the last touches on the holiday decorations. While we were still closed to the public before the holiday gig tomorrow, I called to make sure the caterers were ready.

Check.

I phoned to make sure all was ready for the cast with the slimmed-down version of *A Christmas Carol.*

Check.

That left a pretty wide gap in my day except for a little bit of this and that. I hummed as I sorted through bills to send to the mansion's accounting firm.

Check.

It was so peaceful, I almost forgot about ghosts, paranormal, and murder. It was refreshing.

But as soon as I crossed off my work responsibilities, the dark thoughts of what had happened to three murdered people nagged at me. To that end, I planned to interview more of the guests who had been at the gala. I decided to hedge my bets and speak to the doctor. He was one of the least likely to have killed Allie Campbell-Stone, but he may have seen something. Maybe he would be like Helen, who remembered something after I'd pushed her a bit more. So I looked up the doctor's residence and hit a dead end. He used his office as his address. Picking up the work phone, I called and scheduled my annual appointment. After all, he was an OB-GYN. There was more than one way to get to see a physician.

I left work a little early to pick up my car. We didn't have to cash out at the end of the day since the volunteers were decorating and the mansion was closed to the public; Molly had been upstairs reading merchandise catalogs when I had walked into my office. The volunteers had been gone for an hour. Molly had offered me a lift to the dealer so I could pick up my car, and I'd accepted. After I picked up my car, I headed over the Burnside Bridge and made my way to Sellwood without too much traffic trouble. The commutes were often newsworthy in Portland. *Oh, well,* I thought, *you can't stop progress.*

I stopped for some fresh Como bread at Grand Central Bakery in Sellwood. I wasn't sure what else Danny and I would want for dinner, but it was a start. I had my loaf under my arm as I passed Tilde, a store with purses and earrings—well, I'd lost my silver hoops, and they were sorely missed—and I spotted some big hoops I liked. Out came the emergency Visa again. *Jewelry is my Achilles' heel.*

The dangling posts were in my bag when I walked past a new age crystal and medium reading shop and decided to go inside. I perused the selection of crystals and picked up some rose quartz, always good to keep the heart open to love. Since I was in this relationship with Danny, I thought a boost from a crystal might help. At the cashier counter, I saw a sign for readings. Now, I hadn't had an *official* sit-down reading by another psychic since I'd seen Nora, my relative in Ireland. And since I seemed blocked—and I'd been drawn to the shop—I figured it was a good sign for a consultation.

"She's in," the cashier confirmed when I inquired.

There was a velvet curtain in dark blue that, when pulled back, revealed a table and the woman psychic with a deck of cards.

Technically, since I'd started to see Mac, I guess my title had shifted more toward medium than psychic. Inside the cocoon of the room with the medium, I settled into the chair across the table from her.

I decided to be nonspecific. "I'm here on a whim," I said.

She shuffled and had me cut the cards; then she placed them on the table. "I'll look at the cards and see what they say."

There was the nine of spades that caught my attention, and she kept glancing at it like it had significance. "You're worried about something," the medium said.

It was pretty safe to predict. I was worried about a permanent place to live, three people dead, and a Scottish Highlander spirit appearing whenever he wished.

"Finances?" she guessed.

Having used my emergency Visa card for clothes, I could argue that I was worried about money, but not like I had been when I was living in Sedona, working at the theater, before Aunt Thelma left me half of her estate.

Her eyes kept glancing to the nine of spades.

"What is that card known for?" I asked.

"It's the death card."

I sucked in air. "People have died recently," I said.

Her face lit up. "Aha." She was satisfied that the nine of spades had a reason to present itself besides my financial worries. "Let's see if there is anything from the people on the other side who wish to communicate."

She shuffled the deck again, had me cut the cards, and laid out three more cards in a column.

Just then, Mac appeared behind her. *Coincidence? Kismet?*

"There appears to be a person or persons who wish to converse with you." She was concentrating hard on the cards as Mac smiled at me. "I think it's someone who knows something…I think it's a he…and that he wants you to know something."

I had a hard time keeping a straight face. Mac was playfully twisting the fringe on her shawl and pointing to himself as the one who wanted to liaise.

What a tease.

My card reader put down a few more cards. "There's something about his past that has played forward to the present." She looked to me for a sign. Mac had taken out his blade and was throwing it up in the air and catching it. Anything to make me crack into a laugh, but I dug down into my theater training and remained neutral—well, as much as I could with a psychic medium reading about my life and a Culloden ghost playing with his dirk like he was a juggler. "Well," she said, "I feel his presence in the room."

Of course she does. And I also sensed that Mac had a part to play in my future. What it was, though, remained stubbornly hidden for now.

At New Seasons I bought onion, celery sticks, garlic, chicken breasts, parsley, and noodles. I got to Danny's place before he was home and began to cut up the chicken and vegetables. I tossed everything into the pan and let it simmer in butter. It smelled divine. Aunt Thelma had taught me a late-in-the-day version of chicken soup. After it cooked down, I tossed in some parsley and rice and turned it to a low temperature for the flavors to marry.

The bread from Grand Central was on the counter, and I took out two glasses and filled each one with a merlot. Karma looked at me, hopeful about the soup, so I filled a dish with her kibble and then took a bit of the cooked liquid and poured it over her dry food.

Once it was cool enough, I gave it to her, and she gulped it down in a truly Labrador way of eating. I wondered if she even tasted anything since it disappeared so fast.

After that, we went for a quick walk.

When we got back, Danny was home, looking fine. It didn't take long for us to reconnect and put some more frosting on the cake of our relationship, and it was a lot later when we finally broke bread together and ate soup before slipping into the bedroom for the remainder of the evening.

The next morning it was a clear, cold day for the event. I'd hired some temporary traffic help to manage the cars coming up the road and parking—hiring the same people who'd been used the year before by the mansion, college students and teachers on break and needing some extra spending money for the holidays. We also had volunteers working the event, and then there would be Molly and me, plus the whole board of directors, the caterers, and the theater troupe. Peace, Bryce, and Danny would be here to make sure there were extra sets of eyes in and around the house. In other words, I thought I had this covered. No repeat of the night of the gala.

Even Mac showed up as soon as I'd taken off my coat and sat down to scan through my emails. Interrupted when the caterers arrived, I reminded them to make sure the kitchen door was closed and locked at all times as I looked at their faces. While I recognized several, there was nothing matching Helen's photo, although that person had been hiding in the shadows. *Note to self: Look to dark corners for clues.*

I sighed. Well, my tea reading had informed me that this was not going to be easy. Mac came with me, following around like a rat terrier on an old-time farm. The best I could make out over his appearance and apparent attentiveness was that he wanted attention or maybe he'd broken up with Nina, his pizza house ghost girlfriend. Well, he was one more soul on board for the holiday party.

When it was eleven o'clock, the porte cochère doors opened for the first wave of holiday ticket holders waiting to get inside. Molly was stationed at the podium ready to let them in; I planned to take over in a few hours for the second half of the day.

Red, green, silver, gold, glittered, and ugly Christmas sweaters—you name it, and people were wearing it for the festive day. I had on my cute little plaid skirt, the short black boots, my black leggings and sweater, and Christmas-red lipstick on my lips. I'd even found a pair of Christmas-ornament earrings at the museum store the day before and snapped up a pair with my discount to use as encouragement for Pittock guests to buy merchandise. Sales were forecasted to increase by a wide margin, a high bar posted by the board of directors, but it was possible with the store's fresh and new seasonal offerings.

As I made my rounds through the house, the comments I overheard about the decorating were extremely favorable. I planned to have a thank-you luncheon for the volunteers at the end of January since the mansion would be closed for almost the entire month for the once-a-year deep cleaning.

Upstairs in Henry's bathroom, I saw smiling guests. However, as I peeked behind them into the winter wonderland created by the volunteers, I noticed that the bathroom window was now ajar, bringing in a cold gust from the crisp weather outside. With the magic touch of understanding the old house, I clicked it shut and locked, but I suspected a ghost would open it again.

Back through Henry's bedroom and into the upstairs hallway, I smiled at the mistletoe over the formal portraits of Henry and Georgiana Pittock. *It would have been great to know them.* Just then, I spotted Peace, dressed in a bright-red dress with green leggings. Actually, Peace is one of the few people who can pull off that sort of combination. Her tattoo boyfriend was with her, and they were holding hands.

"I'm glad you made it," I said.

I segued their attention by pointing to the view of Mount Hood outside Henry's bedroom. While her tattoo boyfriend was distracted, I took Peace's hand, purportedly to show her the ice-skating rink that had been transformed from Henry's foot soaker. En route, I whispered, "Do you sense any ghosts?"

"Just that handsome Highlander," she said in a whisper back to me. Mac appeared in Henry's shower, fiddling with all the showerheads and nobs. Lucky for me, he didn't turn the water on—I didn't think he could do it, being transparent and all, but Mac was a quick study and persistent, as I'd discovered in Scotland.

"Well, keep a third eye open or whatever or however you detect spirits. I'll let you know if my psychic alarms go off, but you know everything isn't working for me."

"Your friend who owns the tatt parlor is coming back at the end of January," Peace said. "Gary told me."

"Well, I'm grateful I have you, Mac, and Danny to help me now," I said. "I'm off to check on the caterers."

I hustled down the flights of stairs to the basement level, where I surveyed the food crew in the circular game rooms. Everything looked perfect. Wine was flowing at the station in front of the elevator. I'd made the decision to keep the Otis out of order for today's event. The Dickens stations of Christmas were about to begin.

Heading toward the back room, I checked the caterers' door. It was locked tight.

That's when I bumped into Helen, who had volunteered for this gig. I found her in a Victorian costume, ready for her performance. I grabbed her hand. "If you have a few minutes, will you please check out the caterers? See if you recognize the shadow-person from your photo or if something jogs your memory from the night of the gala."

She nodded and went off on her sleuthing caper. I grabbed a glass of pinot gris from the wine bar. I was supposed to mingle with the guests. Just then, I felt a tap on my elbow.

"I'm liking it," a man said to me. He was dressed in a dapper suit with a plaid cap. He looked like he could be herding sheep with a border collie. I knew him as one of the board of directors for the mansion. "Nice that you added the theater to the holiday event."

After a short parley, I excused myself to check on the main floor. The actors for the Ghost of Christmas Past were ready to go in the library. Now I had a second chance to prove my mettle as the event and theater planner, along with interim curator.

A crowd gathered outside the two interior library entrances, already enchanted by the familiar Dickens classic. I stifled a shiver but wasn't sure why. When I looked up, I saw someone else had come to the performance. This woman was wearing a red dress and smelled like Parisian perfume. It was a soft scent, but definitely there. I could also see through her.

Peace came over to me. "The cheap perfume ghost is here," she said.

"I can see her this time. It's Lucy Pittock. I recognize her from the vintage photographs we have of her. I suspected there was something going on, with Henry's bathroom window open again."

Danny came up behind me, and the three of us moved toward

a quieter portion of the mansion—the coatroom. "Do you see the ghost?" I asked him.

"No. You mean there's someone here besides your Highland ghost?"

"There's a gaggle of ghosts in this old house—mostly family—if I'm not mistaken," Peace said.

"I don't see that Lucy's doing any harm, although you might want to see if you can get any information from her when she's out of the room with the play going on."

Peace agreed.

"I'll keep sweeping the rooms. Just in case anything comes up," Danny said and left through the only door to the coatroom.

I pinched my checks to put some color back into my face. "I thought I saw the OB-GYN who was here the night Allie Campbell-Stone died," I said. "I'm going to see if I can talk to him, and if Mr. Crookshank shows up, I'd also like to speak to him. But right now, I'm off to check in with Bryce and see how things are going outside."

There was a steady flow of guests coming in and out of the house, with the second wave of invitation-only guests now arriving. The plays were choreographed to run through the three ghost acts and then repeat again after the new arrivals had a chance to get their wine and food.

I grabbed a spare coat from the coatroom and headed toward the museum store. We had one of our most trusted volunteers working in the shop since we were short-staffed. *Less than ideal.* Inside the store, guests were stocking up on ornaments, museum magnets, toys—the wooden yo-yos were hot—and puzzles and games. *Splendid.*

That checked, I walked the grounds and found Bryce eyeing the now-closed admissions bay. I knew he was thinking about the apartment.

"How is it out here?" I asked. A cold gust of wind caught me, and I shivered, even with the warm coat.

"Fine. Do you know when we can move in?"

He wants me to wave a magic wand and make it happen. But isn't this the holiday season for wishes?

"There's a board member here now," I said. "I'll see if I can get the okay."

I retreated toward the warmth of the house.

Inside, it felt like I was entering a warm cocoon. I zigzagged through the house and caught up with the board member watching the Ghost of Christmas Present. I didn't want to interrupt, so I went downstairs to see how things were going with the new arrivals and planned to check back with him later.

I spotted Mr. Crookshank with a glass of red wine in his hand, a bombshell of a blonde on his other, and Mrs. Crookshank nowhere to be seen. I could see that Mr. Crookshank had moved on and the reason for the divorce was now hanging on his arm.

I got a refill of my pinot gris and made my way to the couple. "Mr. Crookshank, good for you to be here," I said and extended my hand.

"Wouldn't miss it," he said. "I was just telling Annabelle here"—he nodded toward the buxom blonde—"that the last time I was here, there was a murder."

I grimaced at the reminder. "It was a sad night," I said, trying to understate the gravity of a body stuffed into the dumbwaiter like a prawn.

The buxom blonde had a high-pitched Southern twang. "Portland's mighty rich," she said as she surveyed the opulent holiday decorations. "It's like the Biltmore Estate," she added before she left to get small plates with food.

"I've heard that before," I said, adding to the small talk. "Mr.

Crookshank, I'm curious about the night when Allie Campbell-Stone was murdered." I'd dropped my voice. "I wondered if you had noticed anything—maybe about the catering crew?"

"The food was good," he answered as he took a bite of a crab appetizer from the plate his date brought him. "I like the spread you have today," he added. "But to your question, I didn't notice anything—except a scream, of course."

"Where were you when you heard it?" I asked. "The sound is wacky in this house."

Blonde bombshell excused herself to watch one of the Dickens ghost performances. Mr. Crookshank turned his eyes to watch her backside leaving. I had to admit, she had an hourglass shape. I could understand why Mrs. Crookshank was drinking gin and tonics midday.

"I was—well, I was…" He stopped to clear his throat in the way people do when a situation is uncomfortable. "Well, you see," he began again, "Mrs. Crookshank and I had a little argument about that Campbell-Stone woman. I knew her as the realtor from some of my development holdings."

He was interrupted by a squeal from the buxom-bosomed blonde. "Oh, come see." She encouraged us to look up and pointed toward a paranormal image floating in the air; it was Lucy Pittock. I grabbed the blonde bombshell by her French-manicured hands.

"You see it?" I asked.

She squealed again. "Oh, yes! How do you make her look so transparent?"

"The lighting," I lied.

Crookshank apparently couldn't see the prankster poltergeist.

"You don't see it?" I asked Crookshank to confirm my hunch;

I could tell he was aghast because his date was pointing at the air and he saw nothing. "It's a special kind of lighting used in theater," I said, placating him. "Certain people see it." It was a bold lie, but it popped out of my mouth and seemed to satisfy Mr. Crookshank. "Enjoy the performance."

I went to find Peace to see if she could get Lucy Pittock to disappear, or even better, if Peace had learned something that could help solve the murders. I took the marble steps two at a time and found the same tweed-capped board member on the main level talking to a group of older patrons. He saw me and motioned me over to him.

"Here are the other board members," he said as way of an introduction, since I hadn't met them all before.

Now didn't seem like the best time to ask for my favor, but with everyone gathered, I spontaneously pitched my proposal. "I plan to clean the apartment above the garage and move into it along with a friend for extra security." Lucky for me, there was a quorum present. Tweed cap made the motion with a nod, and the others, swept away, said, "Aye."

"Thank you," I said.

With that, I made a sweep through the kitchen, looking for Peace. She and her boyfriend were there, admiring the view. I took her by the elbow, and we slipped into the butler pantry. Over the original sink, I spilled the news about Lucy. "She just flew through the air, and the blonde on Mr. Crookshank's arm can see her."

Peace looked at me in surprise. "She's got some paranormal radar." I could see that Peace was musing about another potential psychic in the house. "I'll see if I can get Lucy to communicate why she's appearing."

Peace exited through the dining room and into the hallway, toward where I'd last seen Lucy. I hoped Peace wasn't going to use an aluminum foil hat to chat, but beggars can't be choosers, and I didn't know too many people at my disposal who could communicate with the spirits.

Peace's tatt boyfriend was now examining the vintage oven in the kitchen, so I turned my attention toward finding Danny. I started to head upstairs, but before I got to the marble staircase, I spied the banker who had been at the gala the night that Allie Campbell-Stone was killed. He was with the same white-haired—and age-appropriate—woman whom he'd been with the night of the gala. His wife, I presumed, but experience has taught me caution in regard to making assumptions about relationships.

"Hello," I said and reached out to shake his hand. "We met the night of the Crime and Dine gala. I hope you are enjoying to-day's festivities." I kept my smile crisp and hoped my red lipstick was still on my lips.

The banker was the quiet type; I'm not sure about personalities who don't show their cards, but I recalled that this couple had been in my field of vision when I'd heard Allie Campbell-Stone scream the night of the gala. Maybe they had seen something but didn't realize it was important? Each was empty of wine and food, so I segued the conversation toward nourishment to fish for information. "Have you tried the appetizers? And by the way, would you let me know how you like them?"

"We're both vegans."

I made a mental note. "Is there anything that stands out on the menu or with the staff?" I asked. "There are some vegan options. Have you had a chance to try any yet?"

"The vegan-stuffed mushrooms were to die for," the woman said.

The word *die* made me take in some air. "Good to know. And the catering staff—is it as you would expect? And was it satisfactory the night of the gala?"

They both looked at each other, the silent communication between partners. I couldn't tell what they were thinking, so I concentrated on reading their auras. I came up flat. Things weren't working the way they were supposed to, or at least the way they had in the past.

"Well," I said, feeling an awkward moment that seemed to be a code between the two of them, "I hope you have a good day, and I appreciate any feedback. The board of directors wants me to personally connect with our gold-star members." I was really going for the home run of white lies, and I knew it might come back and bite me.

All of that made me want to find Danny even more, to see if he had any counsel. This time I did make it up the marble stairs and saw twice as many guests as had been there earlier. I made a quick sweep through the bedrooms and Henry's bathroom. Sure enough, the same window was open. I went over to it, clicking and locking it into place as I looked outside. I made a mental note to see if I could request Portland Parks to put some kind of pin in it so it wouldn't be able to open anymore.

I found Danny in Lucy's office, where there were two old-fashioned telephones. When Portland first went to the new technology of the telephone, one company had the lines on the west side and one had the lines on the east side—hence the need for two different phones in order to connect with residents on both sides of the Willamette. "The blonde with Mr. Crookshank can see spirits, and it just so happens that the ghost of Lucy Pittock appeared to her. I came up with an explanation, since Mr. Crookshank couldn't see it, but it's a bald-faced lie. Now, Peace is going to see if she can talk to Lucy about her poltergeist pranks, and I'm about ready to trade jobs with Molly, so I'll be at the front podium in case you need anything."

At this point I was breathless from all the running around, and the pinot gris was working on my checks—I could feel the heat-blush rising in my face. Seeing me like this, Danny took me by the waist and kissed me—hard. Well, that wasn't the only thing that was stiff. I gazed into his eyes and said, "Wow."

My stomach was all butterflies, and I felt like I was a teenager again. I'd forgotten what it felt to be head over heels about a man. *How is it that love can make you feel this giddy?*

I saw more than lust in Danny's eyes—I saw love. It was at that precise moment that I heard someone clearing their throat behind me. Turning around, it was a board member. And to add to my awkward moment, Lucy appeared—and Peace showed up giving Lucy a look between amusement and frustration.

I slipped into my most professional demeanor. "Danny is consulting with the Portland police—he's here to make sure things are tidy today."

There was a twinkle in the board member's eyes.

"Please excuse me. I need to take over downstairs," I said.

Lucy disappeared after Peace glared at her, and Peace walked out with me. When we were safely out of earshot, she gave me an update. "Lucy agreed to communicate with me upstairs, in your office."

"Good. Let me know what you find out, and please ask her to disappear for the rest of the day, at least until the guests are gone."

Feeling like I was handling this as best I could, I dashed downstairs to the porte cochère entrance and to the podium. The last round of guests had queued at the bottom of the stairs.

Molly took off to roam the mansion, and I worked the line.

It was uneventful at the podium, greeting and chitchatting with guests until everything thinned out and only a few people milled around, and those who remained were close to making an exit. My feet hurt in my cute boots since I'd been on them most of the day, and I was looking forward to a hot soak in Danny's tub—with him, if I was lucky.

I ruminated a little bit about the love in his eyes when he'd kissed me upstairs, and I knew we were on the path to a serious relationship. The thing that surprised me was that I wasn't putting on an internal fuss over it; in fact, I think I was feeling downright domesticated.

When the last of the stray guests had left, I locked the porte cochère doors and started to make the rounds to turn off the lights. This always took about twenty to thirty minutes to fasten all the windows that may have been opened by guests—or ghosts—and turn off the numerous lights in the house.

I secretly hoped that Molly had started the closing.

Usually I'd begin upstairs, but I wanted to talk to the caterers and see how far along they were with cleaning up their trays and leftovers, so I decided to start in the basement. The long table in front of the elevator had been removed, so I took the sign off the elevator door—*No Service Use*—that we'd placed before the event.

My feet were achy, and the caterers were almost finished. When the last one left the caterers' kitchen, I locked the door and proceeded to walk through the passageway toward the wood fire chute to another door that also entered into the furnace room where we kept our overstock. Locked.

Check.

I retraced my steps, and at the entrance, still inside the passageway, I turned off the lights. Then, I exited that door and locked it.

Check.

The basement, including the game rooms, was tidy and the few chairs that had been set out for guests were stacked and put away. I left the room and made a final check of the ADA entrance to make sure it wasn't propped open and that everything was locked tight.

Check.

The lights were off downstairs. Then a pain shot up through my arch. I slipped off my boots and tucked them under my arm, planning to stow them in my office on the third floor and then finish the other floors. Since my feet hurt, I decided that fitness was going to have to wait, and I pushed the elevator button. I heard the familiar grind of the gears (after all, it was over one hundred years old and still in service) and the *clunk* that announced its arrival.

I slid the first door—like a pocket door—to the left and reached for the interior door made from Honduras mahogany. I stopped for a second when I heard voices upstairs; it sounded like Danny and Peace were still in the house. Opening the final interior door of the elevator, I sucked in air when I saw that Molly was inside, prone and unconscious. I shook her and called her name—no answer—but she was still breathing. Taking my cell phone from my pocket, I punched 911 for emergency services.

Danny and Peace ran up behind me, apparently alerted by my high-pitched voice calling in the emergency. "She's breathing, and the emergency people are on the way. I'm going outside to wait for the fire department and the ambulance while you stay with her." I knew Molly was in capable hands as I dashed upstairs and into the coatroom for my wrap.

That's when I discovered the second surprise of the day. It was Helen—also prone and unconscious but breathing—and I immediately suspected it was another attempt by the sedative murderer.

Calling Danny on my cell phone, I explained my second discovery. While I was talking to him, Peace dashed upstairs to be with Helen while Danny stayed with Molly. It occurred to me that even with extra eyes on the mansion, a murderer had infiltrated the holiday preview; however, I had a job to do, so I went to wait for the emergency responders. First came a fire truck followed by an ambulance. "We found another victim," I said to the first responder. "One's in the coat closet and one in the elevator."

The emergency crews went to work and called for more help. Peace and Bryce helped me sweep the mansion for closing—and to make sure there weren't any more sedated bodies in the house. We turned off lights and closed windows. I collected my bag that I'd locked in one of Henry Pittock's mahogany cubicles, and as I pulled it over my shoulder, I thought about the serious debriefing we had ahead of us. At a bar. With Scotch whisky.

Chapter 19
Debriefing

WE RECONVENED AT THE EASTMORELAND Golf Course Bar and Grill. It's a public course with a restaurant that has a private feel and good food service, and it's usually empty in the winter. It seemed like we needed to get away from the mansion, away from the eyes and ears of Northwest Portland, away from the West Hills and the money associated with it. Now, the neighborhoods that surround the golf course have gentrified, and the cost of a house in Westmoreland or Sellwood is no longer in the middle-class range. The upscale Eastmoreland to the east had always been toney, filled with expensive homes; however, even with the appreciated housing values, the southeast side of Portland feels more casual, a nice contrast to the west side, at least at this juncture when we wanted to talk about what had happened at the mansion.

With relief, we'd learned that the women were okay before the ambulances took them away to the hospital for a thorough diagnosis. We had all ordered shots of Scotch whisky and some food at the bar. Mac joined us as he always did, appearing whenever he wanted. I suspected he missed the amber liquid, but I also believed he wanted to support our group.

"I had asked Helen to look at the caterers before she went on-stage. Maybe she saw something. How long does a sedative take for someone to pass out?"

We were in a heavy review of the events that had transpired over the course of the day. Peace looked over the rim of her shot glass. "About thirty minutes, or maybe longer. It could be that it was slipped to her after the event slowed down. The perpetrator picked out-of-the-way spots after all."

This was true. We had two portable coat racks that were set up on the basement level for guests to hang their coats during the event since we had so many guests.

"I have some good news," I said, deciding to temporarily change the subject and holding up my glass for a toast. "The board of directors agreed to the garage apartment being occupied."

I toasted Bryce.

"*Slàinte.*"

"You can move in as soon as you think it's clean enough for you," I added.

"What about you?" Bryce asked.

Danny and I were getting to that point as a couple where we knew the other's stance without words to each other. "She's living with me," he said as I squeezed his hand. This was all working out for the better. I'd let the board of directors know that an excellent candidate was to move into the apartment.

Peace ordered another round of Scotch. "By the way, I went to your upstairs office, sensed Lucy was there, or at least I smelled the Parisian perfume. She didn't show for the promised conversation, so we'll have to find another way to get her to chat."

Well, she's a trickster.

That thought quickly passed as an order of Angus burgers came, except for me, because I'd ordered the veggie burger with cheddar cheese. After seeing the adorable Highland cows in Scotland, red and black and with horns, well, it was going to be veggie burgers for the rest of my life.

Everything about the day seemed better after the food.

Bryce left after he was content and full of burgers and Scotch, but not so much that he had to call Uber or a cab. He pledged to finish cleaning the apartment and move in as soon as possible. He didn't have much that had survived the fire, so he also planned a trip to IKEA.

Peace left after Bryce. Mac was still sitting next to me, and I could tell he had something on this mind, even as Danny and I were about ready to head home. We planned to have some time in front of the television, maybe pick out a good Netflix movie, and then head to bed.

"Why don't you go find Nina? Danny will keep me safe. Whatever it is, maybe it can wait?"

I said it with kindness. I couldn't imagine how displaced Mac must have felt, out of his time period and out of his country, away from his clan; however, I knew we were somehow intertwined and bound together when he'd followed me to Portland.

What will it take for Mac to rest? Or is he happy here in Portland with Nina?

Chapter 20

Doctor's Visit

I GOT READY FOR WORK—wearing my new black slacks and an ivory top—plus I added my silver hoop earrings and a new scarf in a black-gray-and-hot-pink paisley. I topped it off with the cropped gray jacket and polished my lips with a plum-pink-colored lipstick.

I'd relayed to Danny that I would be late getting home since I'd made a doctor appointment and the doctor was none other than the OB-GYN who'd discovered Allie Campbell-Stone's body with me the night of the gala.

When I pulled into the parking lot at the Pittock Mansion, Molly's car was already there. I'd planned to call and see how she was, but her appearance was a good sign regarding her health. The volunteers would be here soon. Inside my office, I took to the task of emails and was happy to see that one of the board members had sent some résumés over to peruse for new help—two more visitor services representatives to be hired, full-time.

Full-time status was a big deal to me since people need health insurance. I had dozens of résumés to look through. Molly seemed content to work the store and sell admission tickets, although

I noticed dark circles under her eyes. I thought some encouragement was in order. "The sales were great yesterday," I said. Then I took the plunge. "Do you remember anything about what happened?"

She had a pained expression and slowly shook her head. "I was making a sweep through the house, had a glass of pinot gris, was going for the last of the stuffed mushrooms, and that's the final thing that I remember." She looked down at her shoes. "I told the police everything, which isn't much."

"Well, be sure to have your walkie-talkie with you at the store. And good news—we're going to hire two new VSRs, and the apartment over the garage will be occupied soon with someone who will give us some extra security."

She seemed somewhat comforted by that, and as I'd experienced my own share of tragic events in the past, I was too; however, I've learned that dwelling on your personal history—or looking in the rearview mirror—gets you absolutely nowhere. There was no point in being afraid or courting the thoughts of disaster.

The bulk of the day was used to set up interviews. I got three confirmed for tomorrow, and one for the following day. I was ready to get at least one more candidate on the calendar when I received a new email from the board, marked urgent. Opening it, I saw an announcement for a hand-count audit of the merchandise, to be done by an outside firm. This seemed like a good idea—I'd found discrepancies but hadn't been especially alarmed because sometimes there was more stock than the computer showed and sometimes less, but it would be good to get to the bottom of it with an independent company. "So much the better," I said out loud, although I was alone.

That's when I smelled French perfume, the lights began to fade, and there was a high-pitched whining sound—pulsating—and then the shades on the windows began to quiver. In other words, a full-scale poltergeist event. I wished Peace was here.

"You stood up your date with the psychic who could communicate with you," I said to a hazy form that was beginning to materialize in a red dress. "I'm sure you had fun yesterday, spooking Mr. Crookshank's date. By the way, he's a developer who's buying up many properties around Portland, and I don't particularly like him. He's still a suspect in the gala murder. And your father has appeared to me, too, and I sensed that something was troubling him."

I figured that was pretty encouraging. However, my comments didn't seem to resonate with Lucy because she faded away, the lights came back on, and the shades stopped ruffling.

Ghosts can be so picky. Here one minute and gone the next.

It was getting late, and I had the doctor appointment. I heard Molly's voice on the walkie-talkie that she was coming in. We counted out the cash and receipts. Molly had to leave a little early, and I encouraged her to do so with everything she'd been through. I finished up the final accounting and turned off all the lights and locked up the mansion.

On my way to my car, I ran into Bryce with his guitar. "Got the rest of my things," he said excitedly. "I'm planning on spending the night."

My feet were in the stirrups on the doctor's exam room table, and I was looking at some plastic and colorful stick-on fish on the ceiling. The background was painted like the ocean. The décor was oh so clever since that's what you see when you're on your back at your—*ahem*—annual pelvic exam. I hoped Mac wouldn't appear while I was so encumbered. While the doctor was looking into my innermost regions, I squeaked out some questions.

"Do you remember anything unusual at the gala, before we found the body?" I asked.

"Scoot down a little bit more," he said.

The nurse was standing by his side, Pap exam protocol. I obliged and moved my butt toward the edge of the table, feet still in the stirrups, and listened to the crackle of the white tissue exam table paper as I capitulated. *Really, there needs to be a better way to do this.* He took the long swab for the tissue sample, and I knew we were getting closer to being finished. "So, was anything out of the ordinary at the gala?" I asked again.

He looked up at me, my feet still in the stirrups. My toes were cold. My fingers were cold too. *Why are the exam rooms so cold?*

"You can scoot up now," he said. "I remember there was some kind of discussion upstairs, in one of the bedrooms, early in the evening."

He had me sit up on the examination table and then listened to my heart through the slit in my examining gown. "Breathe in," he said.

I complied and then exhaled. "What kind of discussion?"

He seemed satisfied that my heart was working correctly after I'd breathed in and out several times. "There was some marital or relationship discord. I didn't hear enough to call it an argument."

"Do you remember what was said?" I asked. "Did you tell the police?"

"I only caught a few words. Divorce and alimony. As far as the police, I mentioned it to one of the officers that night."

Now he was checking for lumps in my boobs. *It's hard to interrogate a witness when he is manipulating your breasts.*

"Anything else?" I asked, persistent.

"You're due for your annual mammogram. Otherwise, everything looks fine."

"I meant about the food or the catering staff, or anything else unusual that night?"

Standing at the sink, washing his hands, he relented. "There was one other thing. It wasn't a big deal, but I'll give you my impression. I was at the bar with my partner. When the bartender asked for another bottle of merlot—this comment was directed toward the help—the staff member never came back. I switched to a red blend, and I wouldn't have thought about it again, except my partner, who is in the catering business himself, thought it was a staffing issue and mentioned it to me. Otherwise, I wouldn't have remembered it at all."

"Can you describe the person who didn't come back?"

"Well, I'm not sure that I can." He shook my hand. "I'll see you again in a year."

Before I got home, I called Eric Thomson on my cell phone. "Have you heard from Helen?"

"She's taking a day off. Otherwise, she's okay. Grateful that she's alive," he said.

I still felt a little guilty that I'd asked Helen to check things out before she went on with the show, but then I reminded myself that Molly had been targeted too—the culprit wasn't focusing on the actors.

When I got through the front door, Karma greeted me with a wiggle, Danny followed with a kiss, and that made everything feel better.

"All's well," I said. "I interviewed the doctor while I had my exam."

"Kind of figured you'd do that."

I relayed to Danny about the two-word argument overheard by the doctor and what I'd discovered about the caterer who never delivered the red wine to the bartender. "I still think there was someone in the mansion the night of Allie Campbell-Stone's murder who didn't belong."

"Did you see a catering suspect at the preview?"

I thought about his question, replaying the day through my mind. "No, I guess not." Then I thought about one more thing that I had wanted to ask Danny. "Has there been any word about the dueling pistols—pawned or whatever a thief does to get cash?"

"Not yet."

I remembered my tea reading and felt truly blocked, just as predicted.

Danny and I ordered pizza, and after Domino's delivered, we filled out the rest of our evening in the bedroom. Things didn't seem so bad in those late evening hours, with Danny by my side and Karma curled at the foot of the bed.

Chapter 21
Audit and a Pedicure

DRESSED IN MY GRAY PANTS with a cranberry-colored top, I wore my black boots and a cream-colored wrap that I'd found in Sellwood when I'd bought the silver hoops. Early for work, I dug in right away and made the interview appointments for the next day. I had three candidates to interview today, and two more tomorrow. I hoped to make my decision and notify the board by late in the evening the next day.

A representative from the auditing company arrived, announced by one of the volunteers. He wore an impeccable black suit with a green tie and white shirt. Safe, traditional—he looked like he knew auditing. He was bald but had a light, well-trimmed beard. He accepted a cup of Earl Grey tea that I offered and introduced himself as Mr. Smythe.

"The auditing team plans to physically count all the merchandise in the store and in the house overstock. There may be one or two days when the store needs to be closed in order to complete the evaluation," he said.

"I'm glad you'll sort it out, and that will be fine."

"We'll get to the bottom of it," he said. "If there are any discrepancies, we'll let you know."

After he left, a volunteer brought up an interviewee, Grace Benson. She was dressed in a dark-purple dress, the color of Concord grapes, and wore a black hat tipped to one side. Added to the ensemble were caramel-colored leather cowboy boots and a cropped light-brown leather jacket; the whole outfit worked with her strawberry-blonde hair.

In skimming her résumé, I discovered that she'd worked at the Portland Art Museum as a part-time visitor services representative while she finished her degree at Portland State University.

"I'm looking for work related to my history degree. I also have a minor in art," Grace said.

She has an incredible sense of fashion, and I want to see her next outfit.

I asked all the formal questions per the board requirements, taking notes to review, but my intuition was that she was a solid hire. I tried to read her aura but still wasn't able to make that happen, so I'd have to suffice with a background check and her references. She seemed like she would fit in with the museum like a puzzle piece.

After work I met Peace for a pedicure. As soon as we had our feet in the warm, bubbling water, we were both handed a glass of complimentary champagne. We set our massage chairs to vibrate and knead in order to make the muscle knots go away.

"This is the life," I said after a sip. "I still suspect Mr. Crookshank, the developer."

"Why, out of all the suspects?"

"I keep asking myself about motive. Crookshank plays the field, and Allie Campbell-Stone was a high-class call girl when the real estate business was slow. Maybe she threatened to tell his wife, so it was a crime of passion."

I took another sip and felt the knots disappearing under the machine's work.

"Seems like Mrs. Crookshank had a motive too," Peace said. "With an unfaithful husband."

"I suppose you're right. I also meant to tell you that there was some kind of argument between Mr. and Mrs. Crookshank the night of the gala. The doctor overheard two words—*divorce* and *alimony*."

There was a vacant chair, and Mac materialized. He looked at my feet soaking in the water, then took off his translucent boots and put his feet in the empty foot soaker next to me. I reached over and turned on the massage feature of the chair for him. My pedicurist looked at me, oddly, since *she* saw an empty chair, but it was worth it to see Mac's expression when the chair kicked in to vibrate.

"Have you ever thought what it would be like for Shakespeare to come into this time period and hear all the words we speak that didn't exist in his lifetime?" I said to Peace as I thought about Mac, who had a pleasant smile as the massage chair worked its magic. "Some people think the bard's words are hard to understand, but it's because the language has changed. The peasants and the royalty would have understood the meaning in his time. Think about words like *the Internet, vehicles,* and *radio* to someone outside their own time period."

"I run into the same with the aliens," Peace said.

Of course she does.

Peace had closed her eyes as the pedicurist was now applying purple sparkles. Mac looked like he'd fallen asleep in the chair, still vibrating.

"Well," Peace finally said, "if there's something going on as far as the museum and the developer, I'd follow the money."

That made sense. I could sniff around the Pittock accounts, although the bulk of the daily accounting was kept off-site at a private firm. "Maybe I'll talk to Mr. Crookshank again," I said as I had silver glitter polish applied to my toes.

Mac disappeared as a new patron arrived and settled into the chair he'd been occupying. I noted that the new client dripped with diamonds and a Cartier watch, and then I recognized her as one of the gold-star members who'd attended the Crime and Dine gala the night Allie Campbell-Stone was murdered. *Who can forget someone who wears Cartier?* Although for me, I could pull together a great look without the designer price tag. It's all in the creative eye.

Peace was now asleep in the chair, toes spread between the spacers, nails drying. The woman on my other side got a glass of champagne, and the pedicurist refilled mine. I heard light snoring coming from Peace.

"I think we've met before," I began. "I work at the Pittock Mansion, and you were one of our gold-star members at the recent Crime and Dine gala."

If nothing else, I can be persistent. "I'm grateful for this opportunity to ask you about the food and catering. The board has asked me to check in with our gold-star members for feedback, so I'd enjoy hearing what you thought about it, and by the way, I love the holiday-red polish that you picked out."

My silver-glittered nails were drying while the gold-star member's feet were soaking in the warm water.

"The food was passable for a catered event."

Passable for a catered event. I felt a twinge of put-down but plowed forward, still fishing for information that might be useful.

156

"Regarding the staffing, we had mixed reviews, so I'd appreciate your feedback now."

She'd picked up the latest *People* magazine and flipped through the pages.

"It was an off year for the merlot."

It seemed fine to me, but I didn't have the designer palate. I was happy if I could pay my rent and have money for some two-buck Chuck from Trader Joe's. Besides, I was drinking the pinot gris the night of the gala.

"I'll make a note of that," I said. "Anything about the catering staff?" I asked. "I wasn't able to hand out a questionnaire at the end of the gala like I'd planned."

She dismissed it with the wave of her hand. "No, but I was busy consoling a friend who's getting a divorce."

Mrs. Crookshank.

My toes were dry, and I slipped into flip-flops. Getting ready to leave after I'd paid for the service, I realized that Peace's suggestion seemed the most feasible course to pursue. *Follow the money.* To that end, I decided to swing by the developer's fancy office in downtown Portland before work the next day.

Chapter 22

The Developer

MR. CROOKSHANK'S OFFICE was in the pink tower in downtown Portland with a stunning view. Incidentally, on the top floor of the building was one of the best restaurants, the Portland City Grill. I'd heard a rumor that the building had a helicopter landing pad on the roof and that some people used to arrive via that entrance. I didn't know if it was true, but it sure would be a memorable way to get to a restaurant and avoid parking hassles. I bet that gold-star member with the holiday-red toes would have sniffed at such an entrance. Me, I'd put it as a highlight of my life.

By and by, I used my car—and the parking underneath the building—to get a chance to talk to Mr. Crookshank, but I didn't have an appointment. Mac appeared as I got out of my car, and it looked like he'd had a rough night. The best description was *disheveled*.

"Long night with Nina?" I asked as I boarded the elevator. He put his hand to his forehead like he was nursing a hangover. Now, that had me wondering. "She seems so sweet, Mac."

I wanted to know how he felt about Nina, what he knew from his past life, what he remembered, and why he looked like he'd downed a few too many drams.

The elevator doors opened, and I felt the cool air coming from the reception area, stone and steel, modern, with an attractive man behind the front desk. As far as the cold surfaces, it fit, considering Mr. Crookshank liked to take away the warmth of the old and re-place it with new. I don't have a thing against improvements, but some places need to keep their history.

The front-desk man, with the title *assistant* on his desk plaque, looked at me over his reading glasses.

"I'd like to talk to Mr. Crookshank, if possible," I said.

"Do you have an appointment?"

"I don't, but this shouldn't take long. I'd appreciate it if you'd ask for a few minutes of his time." I slipped him my business card.

Mac wasn't playing nice—he was behind the counter with his dirk pointed at the man.

Hangovers make you grumpy.

Mac flipped the man's reading glasses off his nose, marking the first time that I had witnessed something that moved by the Highlander's ghostly hand. The desk man recovered his glasses and balanced them back on his face, not aware that they'd been flicked off by a ghost.

Apparently my Pittock business card opened doors, since I was ushered inside Mr. Crookshank's office. I sat in a chair across from him and surveyed the dark wooden furnishings, juxtaposed with the fresh and large canvas of art on the stark-white wall.

"Thank you for seeing me," I said.

"What can I do for you?"

I swallowed hard and plowed ahead. "When the Pittock Mansion was for sale, after the Columbus Day Storm of 1962, when hundreds of trees were blown down around Portland and the mansion suffered a lot of damage, developers circled around the house and the forty-six acres of property. They wanted to raze it and put in a new subdivision. If it wasn't for the bake sales and teas sponsored by the women of Portland to raise money for preserving the old house, the City would never have ponied up the more-than-matching funds to buy it."

"And your point?" he asked.

"Do you have your developer eyes on the Pittock Mansion estate?"

A vein popped on his forehead. "That's the most ridiculous thing I've ever heard, and I have better things to do than this."

With that, the assistant with the glasses was at the door, ready to escort me out. A twinge of worry came over me, albeit a little late. If Mr. Crookshank knew the right people—or worse, if this was anything like the whistle-blowing that had cost Nina her life in those early days in Portland—it could mean that I needed to polish my résumé. Or pick out a burial plot. But now wasn't the time for me to get cold feet. In Pittock's time and during Prohibition in Portland, corruption was thick as the thieves who profited from it. Dirty cops seized alcohol and transported it to prominent homes outside the area, only to be consumed by Portland politicians on the take.

Where is that corruption now? I pondered that question as I made my way out of the office.

Mac was on the elevator, his features bleak, as was my mood with my unscripted confrontation. And by the time I made it to my office, I was on the phone with Uncle Callaghan. "I think I've done something mildly stupid." I brought him up to speed.

My next call was to Danny. "I told Mr. Crookshank a story about the developers circling the mansion when it was for sale in the sixties," I said. "He denied he was trying to take over the estate, but I think there's something sullied going on regarding the mansion, and not just Allie Campbell-Stone's murder. I think everything is connected."

"I'll see what I can find out," he said. "Be careful."

I had a hot cup of tea on my desk when a volunteer ushered my first interview of the day into the office.

"I see you have experience working at the Japanese Garden," I said to the job candidate.

The garden is a spiritual place in Portland, nestled next to Washington Park. You can walk around and forget your worries as you meditate in nature and beauty, especially in the cooler months, when there are not so many tourists at the venue.

"Yes. I worked the front line, admissions."

While we went over her work experience, I mentally reviewed her outfit. She had on a mustard-yellow top that was quite good with her hair and skin tones. Not everyone could get away with that color choice. She paired it with a black pencil skirt and black boots. Simple, yet pulled together. She had gold balls in her pierced ears, understated but classic. I wrote my impressions on the interview sheet and listed her as a good, solid maybe. The woman the day before had been a for-sure. I was down to one more interview and felt positive that I had two solid candidates, even if the next interview fell short. It was a good thing, because my afternoon interview never materialized.

My two candidates' references were stellar, and I put in a request for the required background checks.

When I was leaving for the day, Bryce invited me upstairs to the apartment for a cup of tea. *At least a ghost hasn't scared him off.*

"It's quiet," he said, sensing what I was feeling.

The apartment was coming along as far as cleaning and furnishing it—he had a couple of chairs and a table overlooking the gardens with an eye toward the path to the mansion.

"I poked the bee's nest," I said and explained my interview with Mr. Crookshank.

"Well, I think someone torched our apartment building. A thirty-day no-fault notice wasn't fast enough."

I agreed with Bryce. "By the way, how's everything with the redhead at the cannabis shop?"

Bryce picked up his guitar and strummed a few chords. "I'm writing our song."

It looked like things were happier for him—a new girlfriend and a place to live. It made my heart feel good.

Chapter 23
Portland's Living Room

Danny and I made our way to downtown Portland for the lighting of the Christmas tree in Pioneer Courthouse Square. The square is designated as Portland's living room, and it hosts carols and a huge fir tree—Oregon really knows how to grow Douglas firs—in the center of the square until the countdown for the lights to illuminate. Portland's living room is also a coagulation of different socioeconomic groups, especially during the day, where downtown office workers and heroin addicts coexist in the same space.

Danny was holding my hand as frosty puffs of breath swirled in the crisp air. We'd had hot chocolate, spiked with a little kick of whisky, before we trekked to the event and were now standing not too close to the front of the crowd.

There was a resounding rendition of "God Rest Ye Merry Gentlemen" from the choir, and for a second my heart flashed to a downtown Catholic church where I'd met a priest who'd saved me after I'd returned to Portland from Ireland not long ago. It's a tightrope, sometimes, to not get lost in the past but keep the lessons learned close to the heart.

I'm at a crossroads.

Danny put his arm around me, and I spied Peace and her tatt boyfriend cuddled together like a couple of doves. This holiday season was turning out better than I expected—Bryce, Peace, and me. And then there was Mac and Nina, two spirits who'd found each other. I thought back to my card reading, when the nine of spades card appeared, but I pushed it out of my mind as the traditional countdown commenced and brought me out of my life review. "Five, four, three, two, one"…and the *ahhs* erupted as the lights flooded the giant fir.

"Let's go home," I said to Danny after I'd absorbed the holiday vibe from the festival. We were on the way through the crowd when I saw the developer, Mr. Crookshank, with one of the board members from the mansion. They were having a heated discussion, loud enough that it captured our attention. We slipped into a doorway, out of sight, but not out of earshot. This board member—I'd only seen him twice—once when I'd interviewed for my original position and when I'd spotted him at the holiday preview.

"We had a deal!" yelled Mr. Crookshank.

"It's off."

As they turned in our direction, Danny took me in his arms, twirled me to the innermost cavity of the door stoop, and kissed me, hard. We avoided being seen, but his kissing made my toes tingle and then parts of my nether regions.

What kind of deal?

At this point, in hindsight, it would have been a good idea to take the time to read the tea leaves, but I made excuses. I had a day off and planned to spend it shopping for more work clothes. I told Danny that I'd be gone for the day for some serious retail therapy. I had several stops in mind—first in Sellwood at a few of the boutique shops, then I'd head over to Southeast Hawthorne Boulevard to get some lunch and finish up a marathon day of merchandise purchasing. Of course, the angst about my Visa card was overruled by the knowledge that I'd submitted a claim to my insurance company and I'd get a check in the mail for the replacement of the contents of my apartment.

I started at Tilde in Sellwood and snatched up two new purses. One was a gray bag, pleather, and carried two smaller bags inside the larger one. *Perfect.* The other bag was brown pleather, a backpack style, appropriate for more casual wear. Oh, and the lining was a muted brown-and-gray flower print. I'd hit the jackpot for bag purchases.

Since I'd concentrated on the basics with the first round of replacement clothes, I now looked for tops that would make everything *pop*—always with a keen eye for adding basics—but only if I found something that I loved. I was determined to put my wardrobe back together in a planned method, although my heart always dictated the final choice.

On Hawthorne I found a place to park on the street. I planned to start on the south side and walk and shop for several blocks, and then make my way back to my car on the north side. This plan also gave me an opportunity to stop at Ben & Jerry's for ice cream, a midday pick-me-up.

Late in the day with shopping completed, I got a call from Bryce. "You might want to come up here," he said. "Lights are turning on and off on the third floor, but it's closed, and everyone is gone for the day."

Lucy the ghost? Mr. Pittock reclaiming his study, my office? Or something else? We didn't have timers on any of the lights upstairs, so whatever was happening…well, it was strange, and it was up to me to investigate. As I headed for Burnside Street, driving was slow-going in the early evening traffic. When I got to the entrance of the mansion road, the gate was still open and I didn't expect to be longer than an hour, so I pointed my car in the direction of the parking lot and curved around the twists and turns.

Maybe Henry or Lucy wants to communicate?

As soon as I was upstairs in my office, I sensed an anxious spirit. I just didn't know which one.

Something is going on here.

The lights were no longer flashing, but the papers on my desk had been swirled around and one of the windows was open. I went over to lock it, and while I was at it, there was a pulsating sound and the furniture in my office transformed into the vintage antiques of Henry Pittock's study, complete with a crackling fire in the fireplace and Henry Pittock's spirit in front of me.

I decided to get right to the point. My luck with ghosts sticking around, except for Mac, hadn't been great lately.

"Is someone trying to take the mansion away from us?" I asked.

There was an oak Woodruff file cabinet, and Henry took out some receipts and a picture of himself in front of the Royal Hawaiian Hotel. I had a Dickens-like moment, thinking about the spirits of Christmas. I thought about Henry's life, having arrived in Portland barefoot and penniless but with the skill of a typesetter. He'd found a job at the weekly paper, the *Oregonian*, and turned it into a thriving business that left him with the money to build his legacy house,

Pittock Mansion. Georgiana Pittock was also built of the same snake hide. She'd been on the Oregon Trail and was swept away by natives, but they went back to trade with her father—a horse for Georgiana. Luckily, the negotiation left her reunited with her family.

I noted a soft ache around Henry's eyes. "So, it's like this, Henry. You were an amazing businessman. You set up your last will and testament and your trusts. You put most of your money toward keeping your newspaper, the *Oregonian*, afloat and left some money to your adult children. But you couldn't have known that the bank was dirty, and since there was no Federal Deposit Insurance Corporation, or FDIC, in those days, the money was lost. It was embezzled and gone. The newspaper kept publishing; however, it's a *ghost* of its former self now, mostly because of recent technology," I said.

At this point, Lucy began to materialize in her red dress.

"The invention of the computer was a game changer for the newspaper business. It started with a machine like a typewriter that could scan copy, and then the big computer monitors came into the newsroom. That made way for the Internet, and news is now available instantly on the computer. We all have them, at work, in our homes, and even our telephones are computers." I held up my cell phone.

"And it's paperless," I continued. "So, the Camas mill that you owned, for your daily paper, became redundant."

Lucy was fully manifested, looking like she had the day of the holiday preview. "Your family struggled with finances after the bank stole the money, and this house fell into disrepair. Your grandson was the last of the family to live here, and he never married, but he had a friend—you probably remember the Ladd family—who loved this old house so much. He encouraged your grandson to sell it to the City."

There seemed to be a calming, and the information soothed the spirits' souls. "So, developers were circling the mansion. They wanted to tear it down, like so many older Portland homes. Your estate, the mansion, is the crown jewel of the old homes that still remain. The developers wanted all the acres that went with it, but there was some good fortune. The women of the era began to raise money to save the old house. By this time there was a giant windstorm and some trees had fallen on the main house; water leaked inside, especially in the hallway on the bedroom level."

A new spirit appeared. She looked just like her portrait in the hallway—Georgiana Pittock. "The Portland Rose Festival is still celebrated every year in June. Georgiana inspired the first festival. And the Waverly Children's Home, which Georgiana started for the orphans whose parents didn't make it across the Oregon Trail, is now part of Trillium Family Services, and is still helping families."

Even with three ghosts in the study, it was calm. "So, the women who held bake sales raised enough seed money that the City bought the mansion and the property in the 1960s. The City hasn't ever released the exact amount of money it spent on the renovation, but the house is back to its original splendor. Some of the original furniture has found its way back to the mansion. The nonprofit Pittock Mansion Society runs the inside of the house. The City takes care of the outside grounds. Several of the trails that you carved through your estate, Henry, are popular hiking trails, enjoyed by urban dwellers and visitors. The Wildwood is one of them. It's a proud legacy toward your vision, but I also have to let you know that there's something untoward going on at the mansion. There have been three murders, and I think they're connected."

The spirits faded quickly, and the modern furniture of my office came back—the fireplace now cold and empty. I heard the reason—the sound of the elevator grinding to the third-floor office. I wasn't sure what to do—confront or hide. I decided to stand my ground, putting my hands on my hips, standing taller, and puffing my chest out to make myself bigger like a betta fighting fish.

When the elevator door opened and revealed Molly, I relaxed, until I saw that she was holding a dueling pistol in her hand—and she had it pointed at me. And then I realized it had been Molly all along, but the loss of my psychic warning system had never alerted me to her. I reached in my pocket for the amulet that Trinity had given me for protection.

"Keep your hands where I can see them," Molly ordered. *Right.* I wished I was packing because I'd be happy to shoot her.

"So, you broke into the gate lodge, took the antique pistols, and made it look like an outside job," I said.

"Turn around," Molly ordered. She pushed the barrel of the pistol into the small of my back, where I knew a small-caliber projectile would do a lot of damage to my innards.

"Get in," Molly ordered me into the elevator. "Second level."

I pushed the button for the bedroom floor. "And, you killed Allie Campbell-Stone the night of the gala. I didn't like her either, but why did you do it?"

The pistol remained solidly in the small of my back.

"Open the doors," Molly ordered.

I capitulated and took a step out of the Otis into the bedroom hallway. The portraits of Henry and Georgiana Pittock watched us, mistletoe still hanging over the pictures.

"And you faked your own attack during the Christmas event," I added, still trying to piece it together. "Why did you need to kill the other two, and sedate the actress?"

She pushed me toward Henry's bedroom, where I could see the twinkling lights of downtown, and then into Henry's bathroom, where the ice-skating figurines were on the Plexiglass, looking festive and happy.

I'm not leaving this world without a fight.

Henry's bathroom window was open, making it frigid in the room. "Do you keep opening this?" I asked, insistent. As if on cue, Mac appeared, standing in Henry's shower where I'd seen him playfully trying to move the knobs before, but he didn't look happy now.

Molly had the gun pointed in my back, and in a fear-filled split second, I heard her squeeze the trigger with a *click*.

The gun didn't fire.

I didn't hesitate. I spun around and punched her, and in those same split seconds, Mac rushed Molly. The pistol flew out of Molly's hand, as if by magic. I looked at Mac, still amazed that he'd figured out how to propel objects.

Molly, disarmed, screamed, "Do you see it?"

She was pointing in the air. What I saw was Nina manifesting along with Lucy and Henry. In hindsight I think I'd summoned a gaggle of ghosts—powered by my now-hot chip, or Trinity's amulet, or maybe both—and the next thing I remember was a collective spiritual rush, and then Molly fell through the open window. I guess she never really believed the stories about the ghosts, but I heard the thud of her body as she hit the dark pavement on the ground level below.

When the police came, I left out the whole business about a gaggle of ghosts in my statement because the cops would have thought I was bat-shit crazy. I told them that Molly and I struggled, and in that tussle, Molly fell through the open window. Bryce had seen most of it from outside where he had a view of Henry's bathroom. He'd gone to investigate when he'd heard the commotion and was worried about me. While he watched, helpless to get inside because he didn't have a key to the main house, he'd called for help. The police found the dueling pistol on the floor of Henry's bathroom, right where Mac had knocked it out of Molly's hand.

Chapter 24
The End and New Beginnings

I HAD TWO NEW EMPLOYEES, and I had to let the volunteers know about Molly. Danny rang to tell me that the Portland detectives found the other dueling pistol, the case, and rambling computer recordings in Molly's apartment. The other pistol had successfully been fired—a rehearsal before she tried it on me—apparently with fresh black powder that she'd purchased locally. The gunpowder in the pistol that Molly had pointed at me was damp—hence, the reason I was still alive. I think Mac saved me, because if anyone knew how to disable gunpowder, it was a Culloden Battlefield ghost.

Danny explained that Mr. Crookshank had spilled his guts to the police as Molly's coperpetrator and coconspirator, and Molly had vented a plethora of personal details in her computer. "She was passed over for promotions—and that's where her jealousy began to fester—even before you were hired. By the way, they found a catering outfit stuffed in a black garbage bag at her place, so it looks like she was the extra catering person at the gala event."

How Shakespearean of her. A disguise. The ultimate tool of confusion used in the bard's plays, right under my own theatrical nose.

"So she slipped a sleeping pill to Allie Campbell-Stone before she killed her," I said. "But what about the scream? Because I was with Molly when I heard it that night."

"At that point, Allie Campbell-Stone was already dead and in the dumbwaiter," Danny said. "Mr. Crookshank confessed that he helped Molly drug and kill Allie Campbell-Stone, and then they both moved her body to the dumbwaiter, without Mrs. Crookshank's knowledge. Later, Mr. and Mrs. Crookshank had an argument about her husband's adultery and a divorce, so that's where the scream originated, and it wasn't Allie Campbell-Stone who screamed after all."

"But it also gave Molly an excellent alibi," I added.

"Exactly. And Mr. Crookshank paid Molly to alter the Pittock inventory to make it look like the mansion was mismanaged, hence a budding burden for the City. Crookshank knew it would take time, but he was willing to wait and use other unscrupulous means to wear the City down and eventually be in a position to buy the property and build multiunit condominiums. Potentially millions of dollars. By the way, Crookshank had his assistant set fire to your apartment complex."

"But why did Molly and Mr. Crookshank kill Allie Campbell-Stone?"

"Once Crookshank got to Molly—and the board member we overheard after the tree lighting—he promised Molly more money than she'd ever expect to see in her life, if his development company successfully got the Pittock Mansion and the estate property. Remember, Molly was disgruntled, and Crookshank needed an inside person. Mr. Crookshank told Molly that Allie Campbell-Stone had found out about their plan and that she had threatened to go to the police if she didn't get a large amount of hush money, so they killed her."

"Mr. Baker too?" I asked.

"Molly killed him because he confronted her the day of the gala about the inventory merchandise discrepancy. After Mr. Baker pointed it out, even though Molly denied it, she feared he was getting too close, or that she would be fired. And Molly had discovered that killing gave her power, fueled by her ambition to get rich. She also learned that by using a sleeping pill as a sedative, she could easily wait and overpower a strong man. When Mr. Applegate fired Anthony Baker, it only bought the curator a little extra time before she acted. Mr. Applegate passed Molly over for a promotion and gave it to you instead, presenting a motive to kill him, all the while feeding her need for power and control, and later, she felt threatened by the actress snooping at the holiday event, so she slipped a pill in her wine, but then worried she'd get caught. That's when she decided to throw off suspicion by taking a pill herself and falling asleep in the elevator."

What a tangled web. "I still don't understand why she saved the dueling pistol showdown for me."

"She'd taken the pistols, case, and all the accessories to throw you in an inadequate light. Molly didn't want you to have success. Then, when you inquired about the inventory and met with a man from the auditing company about a software audit and a physical counting of store merchandise, you posed a bigger threat. When you confronted Mr. Crookshank, she was forced to do something."

I had one other question. "Did Molly steal from the overstock?"

"There was a pile of Pittock museum store merchandise stashed in her apartment."

Well, well. Molly blindsided me. Almost checkmate.

Chapter 25

It's a Wrap

I STILL HAD WORK TO DO, and that included training the two new visitor services representatives. Each showed up on time wearing their own signature style—one with dangling Christmas-ball earrings and a black vintage dress, fit like it was made for her, and the other in a classic white shirt, crisp, with a black pencil skirt and stylish boots. I knew I was going to like both of them.

After everything that had happened, I couldn't help but look forward to a couple weeks off while the house was closed for cleaning and repairs. The audit was still scheduled for the middle of January, and the company was working with the Portland police regarding the merchandise found in Molly's apartment.

After work I met Peace in downtown Portland at the Heathman Hotel. The grand piano was set up for a special event, and when I looked over at the pianist, his hands danced on the keys as he played a Christmas carol. Mac and Nina materialized on the piano, looking into each other's eyes.

"How are things going for you and your boyfriend?" I asked Peace, seeing the love in the air.

"He's coming with me to Sedona." This was the first I'd heard that she was headed home to the red rocks and blue sky. "I've got to recalibrate in a vortex. My alien friends recommended a psychic tune-up. It happens, even to the best of us," she added.

"You know, Peace, mine didn't work well either, but I can't have the chip removed. I'm too fond of Mac. So I'm not going to worry about it for now. My goal is to enjoy a couple of weeks of vacation on the coast. I plan to spend some time with Trinity and Griffin. I owe a lot to Trinity—she gave me the amulet that helped me in the end, and I owe a lot to you too, Peace."

That's when I looked up and saw Mrs. Crookshank coming over to us. "I'm glad you're here," she said to us. Her outfit, a glittered-silver holiday one-piece beauty, was stunning, and she had accessorized it with dangling ruby-jeweled earrings—no doubt the real thing. "My attorney thinks the media coverage will expedite my divorce and I'll get a better settlement, so I wanted to thank both of you."

"No problem," I answered with a smile. "And, if you'll indulge me, the night of the gala, did you scream?"

There was a pause while she fiddled with her earring. "Well, Mr. Crookshank dared me to, while we were arguing. I could never pass on a dare." Just then, the piano player came over and embraced Mrs. Crookshank. He was dark, handsome, and ten years younger. "Got to go," she said with a smile.

"Her aura looks healthy now," Peace said. "There's nothing like getting rid of trouble in your life to make it glow. By the way, who do you think busted up our ghost hunting the first time we went into the mansion?"

"I think it was Molly. She wanted to undermine the inventory on the computer and was using her sticky fingers to boost the merchandise. Later, she brought some of it back into stock, to confuse the issue. She wasn't apt to get caught in the house after-hours, but if she did, she could use the same excuse I'd planned—that she forgot something important in the mansion."

There was still a small piece of the puzzle that I hadn't figured out. "How did the playbill, from the night of the gala, find its way into the underground tunnel?" I asked.

Peace looked up at the piano where the ghostly lovebirds—Nina and Mac—where looking over at us. "I think it was Nina. She'd figured out how to manipulate objects but didn't know how to appear outside the space of her place of death. Mac knew how to appear outside of his death place—Culloden—but hadn't been able to manipulate objects. So I think they taught each other in order to help you. Isn't love great? It can move heaven and earth."

It certainly can.

Acknowledgments

I WOULD LIKE TO THANK Inverness Tours and my guide, Dave Fyfe, for the history and touring around Inverness, Scotland. Culloden was a highlight, and I was grateful to walk the battlefield moor on a chilly, clear April day. The ritual Scotch tasting didn't make it into the book per se, but I explored it firsthand, and those with keen editorial eyes may have noted that *whisky* in this mystery is spelled without the *e*, and in *Celtic Ties* (The Lizzy O'Malley Mysteries, Book 2), *whiskey* is spelled with the *e*, the traditional spelling for Irish whiskey. In Scotland, it's Scotch whisky. When in Rome…

I'd like to thank the Pittock Mansion Society for the opportunity to work at the mansion. I'd also like to acknowledge the Oregon Historical Society for the use of their library. I can't confirm the presence of tunnels at the mansion, although the rumors continue. What I can relay is that the entry road to the mansion changed in the 1960s. When the Pittock family originally lived on the hill in 1914, they would drive their 1912 Pierce-Arrow from the garage, past the port cochère entrance, around the east grounds of the mansion, to the road past the gate lodge. When the entrance road was moved, the forest swallowed up any former work roads and possible tunnels.

Henry's bathroom window and its persistent opening and closing remains unsolved; however, Pittock Mansion has a reputation for being haunted. If you visit Portland, Oregon, see it for yourself—or if you are local and have never been to Henry's house on the hill, I recommend it.

Other thanks to the City of Portland for the foresight to purchase the mansion, and a warm thank-you to the heart and soul of Pittock Mansion, the visitor services representatives and volunteers. I'd also like to thank Carolyn McGreevy, Meg Eberle, and Liz Danek for their assistance.

Please take a few minutes to write a review on Amazon and/or Goodreads. It makes all the difference. Thank you!

About the Author

A NATIVE OREGONIAN, KELLY RUNNING coaxes an appreciation for the English language into irrepressible seventh and eighth graders. Her poetry and essays appear in literary journals such as *VoiceCatcher* and *Faultline*. Earlier in her career, she wrote commercials and press releases for radio. Her passion for research and interest in indigenous spiritualism instills authenticity in her storytelling. *Pittock Mansion* is the third book in the Lizzy O'Malley Mystery series. More information is at www.kellyrunningmysteries.com .

Also by the Author

A Lizzy O'Malley Mystery

MEDICINE
WHEEL

Kelly Running